Marlowe Kana - Volume 1 (Chapters 1-10)

A Word On Sharing:

Please share this book with anyone you see fit.

If you received this book from a friend and liked it, all I ask is that you buy the future volumes and share them with your friends. The individual dollars and pennies don't matter to me nearly as much as being able to write for you. Your financial support is appreciated, but word of mouth is worth 100 times that -- so spread the word, share this book, and keep reading!

Thank you for your support!

Table of Contents

Acknowledgements

Without Beth Watson, Meghan Hetrick, Rowena Yow, Joseph Rhodes, Jason Covert and Casey Edwards, this book would not exist.

For Beth.

1. A Day In The Life Of:
The Millars

"This *can't* be happening!"

She tore through her family's modest two-story home, skidding when her socked feet reached the kitchen floor tile. The lights rose as she crossed the threshold. Displaying the agility of her hero Marlowe Kana, she nimbly dodged the corner of the kitchen island and barely slowing, extended her hand and reached for the door handle to the greenhouse. Cool, fresh air greeted her shorn scalp as she flung the door wide.

"Dads!" she yelled.

Brian and David Millar both looked up, jarred from the peaceful zen of tending to their plants. Before either could ask what was going on, Britany blurted out. "It's MK! It happened! She's... You gotta come see!"

Brian looked at David and shrugged. "I guess we should..."

"Of course," David said. "It's important to her."

"Well, it's important, period," Brian replied. "But especially to her."

The fathers carefully laid their gardening implements on the table and walked toward the door, removing their gloves and masks. Britany had already fled back inside, finding it physically painful to be away from the screen. As Brian and David entered, they were taken aback by the massive red bar flashing across the screen on the living room wall as it blared the word "GUILTY!" Above the text was a pair of side-by-side photos of the most famous person in the nation: Marlowe Kana.

The left-hand photo displayed a half-body shot of a healthy, muscular woman in full MilSec dress uniform, campaign ribbons and medals adorning nearly the entire top half of her jacket. She had short white hair, carefully groomed and parted in a manner befitting a by-the-books MilSec soldier. Despite the massive scar across her cheek under her right eye, there was a light and a life in her eyes that complimented her slight smile. Her expression spoke volumes. It seemed to say that, while she took her duties seriously and performed them with the gravity of a committed and dedicated soldier, she had, in fact, a truly all-encompassing love for her work. A fact that all of her 20+ million fans knew from watching her Feed, despite her seemingly constant annoyance at the fame it brought her.

The right-hand photo showed the same woman, her hair shaved to stubble and her uniform replaced with a bright orange prison jumpsuit. The smile was gone, as was the light in her eyes. They seemed dead and hollow. Her cheekbones were pronounced and her face was gaunt from malnourishment.

The NewsFeed crawl below the photos detailed that just moments ago, at 7:02 p.m., "Next Top Soldier" Hall-of-Famer, Major Marlowe Kana, had been found guilty of attempted murder, conduct unbecoming a MilSec soldier, and treason against the United American State.

Despite having seen many hyperbolic developments on the NewsFeed in their days, both David and Brian couldn't help but gasp. The national hero — everyone's favorite Next Top Soldier for the past ten years and the General's daughter — guilty of treason? It seemed impossible to believe. But there it was, writ large on the wall-sized screen, with every talking head on the NewsFeed animatedly discussing this latest development in the saga that had gripped the nation for the last three months.

"Oh dear," Brian said just as David blurted out "Oh shit." Brian smacked his husband on the arm.

Through the haze of her dismay, Britany heard her father cursing. She didn't bother to remind him to put a credit in the curse jar. Self-improvement seemed trivial in the face of such earth-shattering news.

The street light streaming through the window wall glinted off of Britany Millar's tears. She looked up at her fathers. Together, they went to her and comforted her. They ached to explain that even heroes can screw up and that everyone must be beholden to the law. But they couldn't find the words. They didn't need to. The entire nation had flooded the Feeds with their responses.

"...That's right, Tom," Amanda Stokes, correspondent for NewsFeed, was saying on the screen. "The nation overwhelmingly believed that Marlowe was guilty all along, with #IKnewIt in first place with 12 million tags."

"You called it from the beginning, Amanda," Tom Wallace replied, "For weeks, we've been watching #IKnewIt trend upward, as the evidence proving Marlowe's innocence never turned up. So that is no surprise. But MK still has her fans, as we can see by the second place response #MarloweIsInnocent, followed by #PrayForMarlowe, #FuckMilSec, and #ShavedHeadSolidarity..."

The screen suddenly went silent as Britany extended her hand and circled her index finger counter-clockwise; a gesture-based command relayed to the screen via the embedded Pod that wrapped around the base of her skull, which muted the Feed. In a voice strangled with pain, she summoned the omnipresent AI assistant, JAQi.

"Yes, Britany?" JAQi replied flatly, seemingly from nowhere and everywhere at once.

"Post to my Feed that I'll never, ever believe that MK is guilty, and anyone who does is immediately banned from my list!"

4

"Yes, Britany," JAQi replied. A tone signaled that the job had been done.

"And also that I'm NOT growing my hair back just because she lost! Not ever!"

"Yes, Britany," JAQi responded. Another tone signaled.

"And--"

"--Britany, honey..." her father Brian interjected soothingly.

"No!" she snapped. "This isn't...I'm NOT apologizing for supporting MK!"

"Honey," David chimed in, "We know..."

"It's a setup!" she yelled. "It has to be! Marlowe would never...she didn't do this! It's the terrorists! It's got to be! They're setting her up!"

"It's a really complicated--" Brian began to say, before David cut him off.

"You're right, honey," David consoled. "This is a tragedy. You have a right to be upset." He turned to his husband and looked him in the eyes. "We all do."

On the screen, aerial footage flickered of Marlowe being led into a large secure transport vehicle, while the crawl continued to repeatedly trumpet her guilty verdict. Brian Millar hugged his daughter closer, and placed his free arm around his partner's shoulder. Nothing would ever be the same: if they couldn't put their trust in Marlowe Kana, then in whom could they?

Together, the family began to cry.

2. In With A Whisper...

Marlowe's ass was numb.

She had been perched for the last hour on a cold metal bench bolted directly onto the side of a cold metal transport truck. And naturally, she was seated directly over the back wheel well, where the vibrations of the road were magnified. Her wrists and ankles were bound together with large, magnetically sealed cuffs constructed specially for abnormally strong, augmented super-soldiers. Both sets of cuffs were chained to the other in such a way that Marlowe was unable sit up straight or even stretch her sore, weakened muscles. The fact that the orange prisoner's jumpsuit she was wearing did very little to insulate her rear from the frigid metal in the back of the unheated transport didn't help matters.

Add in the fact that she hadn't eaten anything beyond vitamin supplements and water in the last three months, and it meant that Marlowe's numb ass, while annoying, was really just the beginning of her problems.

They could have held the trial anywhere. It would have made sense to do it in Indianapolis, at the Capitol building in MilSec Tribunal High Court. But the powers that be wanted to make a point. So they had trucked nearly the entire judicial operation to Atlanta for her trial. It made for great entertainment on the Feeds. There was nothing more poetic than parading Marlowe around her hometown in a prison transport. All of this was designed to make Marlowe as miserable as possible while entertaining the masses, and it most certainly worked. So she was already uncomfortable when the young and desperately over-eager blonde guard seated to her left opened his mouth.

"I, uh...I watch your Feed," he said.

She didn't look at him. She didn't even look up. She stared at the grated flooring, hoping that counting the squares would somehow make him disappear.

"I've been watching it for years," he continued. "I wish I was old enough to have seen it during your football days--"

"Jacobs," the Sergeant seated across from them barked.

"What?" He replied. "It's not like we'll ever get this chance again, Sarge."

Sergeant Morris rolled his eyes. "You're a MilSec soldier. Contain yourself."

Jacobs did not contain himself. He couldn't. He was tied with at least 20 million other people for the title of "World's Biggest MK Fan". More than half of the United American State's 40 million citizens ranked her Feed positively, and nearly all of them saw her face at least once a day on Feeds, product packaging, service announcements, MilSec recruitment posters... And here he was, sitting shoulder to shoulder with her. He wasn't about to pass up the opportunity to talk with her.

"I just... I have a question? If I may?" Jacobs asked.

Marlowe sighed heavily. She raised her head from between her shackled hands and turned to look at Jacobs. He couldn't have been older than nineteen, which was the only reason she decided to tolerate his puppy-like eagerness.

Jacobs nearly choked. "...Wow. Just...okay, so, I don't really know why you tried to kill Sergeant Corta. I mean, I didn't really watch her Feed ever, but I know a lot of people watched her...but I don't really believe that you were jealous of her. Her ratings aren't that good. She's not even half as famous as you."

Marlowe very slowly and deliberately blinked at Jacobs.

"I mean, I just...I guess you had your reasons? That's not really important, honestly. Not to me. Not as a soldier, I mean."

"...Is there a question somewhere in there, Private?" Marlowe asked.

"...Yes, I just...well, I mean, how did you end up here?"

"I was found guilty of treason against the United American State," she responded. "That tends to land you in the back of a prison transport with a talkative Private."

"It's, uh...Private First Class," Jacobs said nervously. "And, I mean... I get that, but..."

Suddenly, a loud chirping sound echoed through the back of the transport.

"Oh wow!" Jacobs crowed. "I just hit 25,000 viewers on my Feed!"

Marlowe and Sergeant Morris both rolled their eyes simultaneously.

"You installed FeedMeter on your Pod?" Morris asked the young Private. "You know that's against regs."

"Well, I didn't..." Jacobs stammered. "It's just that, when I found out I pulled this detail, I just had to know what it would do to my FeedRank, just being in here. You know...with MK."

Another ding. "Wow! Fifty thousand!" Jacobs exclaimed.

"Great," Marlowe said, "Now fifty thousand idiots know you're a terrible soldier who violates regulations."

Jacobs laughed nervously again. "Well, no...they can't hear us. Mic's muted. 'Prisoner's rights' and all that..."

"Fine," Marlowe said, "But I'm sure they can hear this." She extended her bound hands as far as she could toward Private Jacob's vest camera and flipped up her middle fingers.

Sergeant Morris chuckled. He had always liked MK. But he was MilSec first, as he had been for nearly twenty years. He knew the job, and that it was best not to let emotions (or follower counts) get in the way.

Private Jacobs blushed, embarrassed by looking like an idiot in front of his hero. With a slight creak in his voice, he said "So, uh, I was wondering..."

Marlowe sighed. "What now, Private?"

"It's Private First Class," Jacobs again corrected.

Marlowe narrowed her eyes.

Jacobs ducked his head sheepishly, cleared his throat, and asked "I just wanted to know, you know...how did you get captured? I mean, I've watched your Feed since before I joined MilSec. Hell, you're the reason I joined in the first place! I even used to wear the scar in school!" He lifted his finger to his right eye. "You can even see where the ink stained my—"

"—Okay, enough, Jacobs," Sergeant Morris said.

Jacobs continued, "With your augs...I mean, I've seen you take out ten, even fifteen enemy combatants before! And it's just the two of us back here. You could probably —"

"Secure that line of questioning, Private!" Sergeant Morris commanded.

"And then what would I do?" Marlowe asked.

Morris and Jacobs looked over at Marlowe. "Ma'am?" Jacobs queried.

"I haven't eaten real food in months. I barely have the energy to suffer your inane bullshit right now, much less break out of here. And even if I did, I'd be dead before I left the transport. I'm strong. I'm not bulletproof. So, even though I would love to pop these cuffs and bolt, I can't. And even if I could--"

Jacobs's FeedMeter chirped, interrupting Marlowe. "Holy...one hundred thousand!" Jacobs said.

"...Right," Marlowe said with a sigh. "And then there's that. I would have to kill two MilSec soldiers with one hundred thousand people watching, after swearing for three months that I'm not a traitor. And what would that prove? That I'm totally innocent? That I am definitely *not* a traitor who would murder her own? That everything I've sworn to uphold and protect with my life was a lie?"

She shifted in her seat as much as she was able. The chain that bound her wrists to her ankles jangled. "Whatever... It's all bullshit. The trial...this parade through Atlanta...and especially this conversation."

The transport fell silent. Sergeant Morris cleared his throat. Jacobs tapped his fingers on his leg. Marlowe placed her face back into her palms. The transport hummed as it carried its cargo of one prisoner and two chastened guards.

A distinctly different series of beeps sounded from Jacobs's wrist.

Marlowe sighed loudly. "And what was that? Did you hit the the million viewer mark or something?" she asked.

Jacobs checked his watch. He looked up and grinned at Marlowe. "Nope. It's time to go."

Marlowe's eyes widened as Jacobs suddenly leaped up from his seat and across the truck. His forearm landed across the throat of Sergeant Morris, and his body pinned the Sergeant's rifle against his chest. With one swift movement, Jacobs pulled his sidearm from its holster, placed it against the temple of his commanding officer, and pulled the trigger.

The slim railgun hummed. A metal slug flew from the tip of the weapon. A red mist erupted from the former head of Sergeant Morris.

The transport suddenly lurched, as something hard and explosive slammed into the side of it with a deafening BOOM! Before it could balance out, another explosion hit just inches from where the first landed, followed by a third. The force of the barrage tipped the transport onto its side. Marlowe's back and head slammed against the side of the vehicle. Jacobs crash-landed on his back beside her.

Another explosion erupted outside, and then another. The sound of metal ripping through metal could be heard all around as the lead and follow transport vehicles were picked apart. The barking of orders and screams of death echoed everywhere.

Marlowe struggled up to her knees. She lifted her head to see Jacobs lying upside down, ass in the air, his knees on either side of his head. He was grinning ear to ear. His FeedMeter chirped again in triplicate.

"Now THAT was the million follower mark!" he exclaimed. He rolled to his side and rose to one knee. "You ok?" He asked Marlowe.

She looked at him wide-eyed; her mouth hanging open. "Uh..."

"What? What's wrong?" Jacobs asked, checking her over. "Did you get hit? Are you bleeding?"

"I, uh...I'm fine," Marlowe replied. "What the fuck is--"

There was a vigorous clanging at the rear of the transport. Loud beeping could be heard.

"Stand back and brace yourself," Jacobs told Marlowe as he positioned himself between her and the doors. He had no weapon -- his rifle and sidearm were now useless. A biometrics lockout was activated the second he murdered Sergeant Morris. If this wasn't who he thought it was, he was going to have to fight them with his bare hands.

A blast shook the truck. The right-side door, now facing the bottom, fell open and hit the ground with a loud CLANG. A group of dark-clothed legs and boots could be seen from the opening. Then, the other door was raised up.

"All good in here?" A voice queried.

Jacobs smiled. "Right as rain," he said, as he walked toward the rear doors and climbed out of the back of the truck. He turned and beckoned Marlowe to exit. "Come on," he said.

"Fuck you!" she replied.

Jacobs's mouth dropped. "But...we're rescuing you!"

"I have no idea who you are or what you want with me," she snapped. "Why the hell would I go with you?"

"Well," Jacobs responded, "You were on your way to prison for a crime you didn't commit, and now you're not, thanks to us. Unless you still want to end up there?"

Marlowe weighed her options. It didn't take long; she didn't have any. Reluctantly, she stood and waddled toward the back of the truck. She was helped out on her left by a uniformed female MilSec soldier who had apparently defected. On her right, she noticed a man clad in an unfamiliar pattern of pixelated camouflage, with chest armor that looked like it was made in a garage, and elbow and knee pads purchased from an Imagen Sporting Goods shop.

They helped Marlowe into the back seat of a pre-war vehicle that still miraculously rolled on tires and staggeringly enough, seemed to be powered by an electrical motor. The mercenary took the driver's seat while the MilSec defector joined Marlowe in the back. Jacobs finished a conversation with another squad of four soldiers, half guerrilla and half MilSec defectors. He pointed into the sky. One of the guerrillas raised a rifle and opened fire on several drones that hovered above. They laughed as pieces of metal and glass and circuitry rained down around them.

Jacobs hopped into the front passenger seat of Marlowe's vehicle, and they sped off.

3. The Numbers Are In

A checkerboard of various Feeds spanned across the wall-sized screens surrounding President Cook's desk.

"Does This Prove MK Is A Traitor?" The caption on one Feed asked, as pundits eagerly discussed the attack on the transport.

"More Than Guilty!" another caption blared. The footage of explosions rocking and toppling the transport truck played in slow motion.

"Terrorist Plot To Kill MK?!?" Asked another, as an uncredentialed "terrorism expert" discussed the situation via live chat with a young boy who was hosting a CitizenFeed from his bedroom.

Dozens of other Feeds had dozens of other takes on the trial, the prison break, Marlowe's supposed attack on Sergeant Corta, and even the fashion of the non-MilSec citizens who had ambushed the parade of armored vehicles. One Feed featured a fashion expert enthusing that the guerillas' strange-looking, black-and-white-speckled camouflage fatigues, along with the makeup and masks they wore, would be the hot, must-have look for spring.

Despite three of the four walls of his office being covered with footage from dozens of Feed streams,

President Cook's steely blue eyes were fixed on a small screen at the center of his desk.

"No, go back one frame," he said as he ran his fingers through his salt-and-pepper black hair. JAQi complied, rewinding the video on the screen by a frame. It was a recording of the NewsFeed drone footage. On the screen, the left hand of the solder exiting the prison transport with Marlowe moved slightly farther from his face, his middle finger extended toward the drone overhead.

"This one is perfect," Cook said. "Grab it." The screen flashed white for a fraction of a second as JAQi captured the image.

"The soldier in the image is Private First Class Robert Jacobs," JAQi said, its receptive voice filling the room. "Shall I fetch his dossier?"

"Nah, leave the profiling and investigations up to MilSec Command," the President said as he flattened the hairs he had distractedly ruffled. "Just get this image out there, along with the others in this group whose faces you can see. National alert, every screen, unclosable. And I want to know why some of these peoples' faces are blocked. "

"Absolutely, sir," JAQi said.

"Play it again."

President Cook watched, for the eleventh time, as the prison transport was ambushed by pre-war vehicles. He managed not to flinch as he watched a large cargo truck slam head-on into the MilSec convoy's lead vehicle, stopping it dead in its tracks. Rockets fired from shoulder-mounted launchers flew from off-screen into the maglev drive of the heavily armored prison transport. The resulting explosion of the levitating propulsion engine scorched the road, flipped the behemoth up and tipped it on its side. The turncoat MilSec soldiers from the rear escort exited and opened fire on the soldiers attempting to exit the two disabled vehicles.

Half a dozen armed personnel, clad in parts and pieces of stolen or homemade armor, appeared from off-screen in all directions -- their faces frustratingly blocked out and pixelated on the camera. Teaming up with the MilSec traitors, they joined the attack, using rockets, homemade chemical explosives and biometrically hacked railguns to annihilate what remained of the MilSec guard. Marlowe and Jacobs were helped out of the back of the prisoner transport. The groups split up and entered their getaway vehicles. A soldier lifted his rifle and opened fire on the drone recording the events from above. The screen flickered in rainbow colors for a fraction of a second before going dark.

The President looked up from the screen on his desk. He surveyed the array of Feeds before him and smiled. He rotated his chair to his left and addressed the wall-sized grid of faces watching him; each member of the Board of

Directors of Imagen Corporation was grimly awaiting his reply.

"Well, Steven?" Chairman Alvin Davis asked. "You cannot tell us in good faith that you saw this coming."

"This?" President Cook replied. "No. I didn't see this coming. This is so much better than what we planned."

"What *you* planned," the Chairman countered. "This thing you've concocted is coming off the rails."

"No, this plan WE all signed off on, that WE are enacting... This plan is going far better than WE could have possibly imagined. It's a huge success."

"How the hell do you call this a success!?"

"Look at the ratings!" Cook said, gesturing toward a grid of statistics on one of the Feed displays. "Off the charts, across the board...the entire nation -- forty million citizens -- all of them, engaged as never before! Don't you see the potential here?"

"All I see is a gigantic shitshow!" Chairman Davis replied, his face as red as his necktie. "You've got a multi-million credit MilSec asset -- our biggest ratings gainer, mind you -- running rogue with some splinter group of whoever the hell those people are, doing whatever the hell they plan to do with her...dead soldiers, destroyed vehicles, pandemonium across every Feed...a nation completely folding in on itself! That's what I see!"

Cook sighed. He rubbed his temples. "You know what I see?" His muffled voice asked from behind his hand.

"Why don't you enlighten us," Davis said drily.

The President removed his hand from his face, clenched it into a fist, and slammed it on his desk. "I see an old man doing business the old way!" He barked. "Lazy and myopic...no understanding of what drives people! Of what drives engagement! I see a group of suits who have grown complacent, who can't see the bigger picture."

"Watch yourself," Davis warned. "Your pedigree betrays you. Yes, the office of the Presidency cannot govern Imagen Corporation operations, and vice-versa. Your father saw to that. He was a wise man. He understood the benefits of divisions of power. And when he was the Chairman of Imagen, he oversaw the greatest rebuilding and revitalization of a country that this world has ever seen. And although you won the popular vote, you are still beholden to the agreements struck between the new constitutional council and this company."

"I won it over you, I might remind you," Cook retorted.

"Yes, as we decided," Davis replied without hesitation.

Cook sighed and rolled his eyes.

Davis continued, "Your father did not intend for his rogue egomaniac of a son, drunk on his own power, to run rampant and undo all the work he completed when Imagen had provisional control over the nation. He intended for the office of the first President of the United American State and the Board of Imagen Corporation to work together to continue his goal of Reformation. He was a man of great vision. You, however...you weren't even alive the last time this country had a president! You are your father's son, yes. But you're absolutely *not* your father."

"You're right," Cook said. "I am not my father. I am the President of the United American State, goddammit!"

"Steven --"

President Cook slammed his fist on his desk, stopping Davis cold. He stood up from his chair, defiantly facing the Board. "I am the first President this nation has had in 54 years, since before the war!" He barked. "The people trust in me, just as they trusted in my father when he was in your position, 'Chairman' Davis!" The emphasis on *Chairman* caused Davis to grit his teeth.

Cook continued, "He recognized the need for a leader that doesn't belong to a corporation that employs the people of this nation. And the people want someone who represents *them*, and not the interests of the company that produces everything they have and use. They need a man that is of the people and for the people, elected by the people -- and goddammit, that's what I am!

"Steven, if you'll just --"

"--And if the engagement metrics on the Feeds from tonight and from the past three months are any indication, I am doing the job granted me by the people of this great nation! Now, if you'll excuse me, ladies and gentlemen of the Board, I need to address the Citizens -- my employers -- about the events that have just unfolded."

"Steven!" Chairman Davis said, just before his Feed was cut off along with the rest of the Board members'.

President Steve Cook sighed heavily as the lights brightened and the wall screens faded to white. He closed his eyes and inhaled deeply through his nose. He counted to ten, and then slowly exhaled through his mouth. Centered and calm, he approached the doorway of his studio. It slid open as he walked toward it.

"Marcus," he said, addressing his assistant who sat just outside the studio.

"Sir?"

"I need you to personally create a FeedRelease announcing an emergency CookTalk. Make it public...general admission based on the Citizen Lottery System. Doors open at nine p.m., I'll begin speaking at nine-thirty. Make the slogan something like…'Back To The Top.' and make sure the word 'Top' is underlined. Three times. The fans will love deciphering that."

"Yes, sir," Marcus said. He gestured his hands upward and began typing on a light array that appeared before him. "That's a very short turnaround... Do you need me to page the writing staff?"

"No, I've got this one. Any vital messages?" President Cook asked as he made his way briskly toward the exit.

"Well, Chairman Davis called back the second you hung up on him, but I'm sure you expected that."

Cook nodded. "Anything else?"

Marcus scanned his other screen. "A few Anons claim to have information on Marlowe's whereabouts...none appear credible. One just says 'Post your Ballsack.' And the dancing cat GIF you liked is back again."

Cook rubbed his chin pensively. "Reblog the cat. Ignore the rest."

"Yes, sir," Marcus answered as the President left to address the nation.

4. The Best Laid Plans...

Marlowe felt the weight of the magnetically locked cuffs that wrapped around her wrists and ankles. She felt the heft of the cable that connected the restraints and kept her from standing completely straight. She felt the strain of every single muscle fiber in her body, both natural and augmented as they sagged, heavy from malnutrition and fatigue. She felt her head throb with every weak heartbeat. Her eyes pulsed as the capillaries expanded and contracted.

She could smell propellant and gunpowder on the soldiers who rode along with her in the truck -- scents that she remembered during her tours overseas in the Gaslands, fighting the many terrorist organizations that threatened the United American State's way of life. Smells that could only come from black market weaponry used by deserters who had turned against the organization she spent her adult life serving, to rescue her from a prison sentence for a crime they believe she didn't commit. As a loyal MilSec soldier, she should despise them. But on that same token, they were the reason she was in a civilian vehicle and not sitting in a jail cell in the Citadel. Why they were helping her, she didn't know. Maybe they were terrorists, or maybe they were just an overzealous faction of her fan club. Marlowe surmised that when you're surrounded by strangers with guns, confined in binds and completely malnourished, there was very little difference between a rescue and a kidnapping.

But at least her ass was no longer numb.

Her thoughts began to drift as she contemplated the events of the past few months. It seemed to her that the chaos of her current circumstances was a natural progression of her entire screwball life. Even from a young age, it felt to her like every single shortcoming of hers had been on public display. As an "illegal child" -- a child of a non-native Citizen -- adopted by a revered MilSec General and his celebrity actress wife, Marlowe faced immediate and overwhelming fame and was put on every gossip-related NewsFeed from babyhood onwards. And of course, it ensured that her childhood became a highly rated Feed show.

Her early draft by the UAFL at age fourteen made her a celebrity in her own right, until she was banned from the league in the middle of her third year for "undisclosed augmentations" -- which had come as a shock to her, since she'd always presumed her uncanny speed and strength were simply the gifts of talent and genetics. No one had ever thought to test her for nanofiber muscular augmentations, because no one knew that they even existed.

If it wasn't for the full-body scan she was subjected to on the return trip home from an exhibition game at the island resort in Oz, they probably never would have. A measure typically used to detect terrorists and their smuggled weapons ended up nearly bankrupting the

League after allegations of Marlowe's augmentations being purposely covered up for ratings ran rife.

To discover she was an Aug through a SportFeed press release was crippling, and not knowing how or why she acquired them made life downright debilitating. Depression and a suicide attempt kept her out of the public eye until she was eighteen, when she was finally able to enlist in MilSec,one of only a few hundred non-criminals to willingly serve, which itself was NewsFeed worthy. It was one of her father's better ideas. Her subsequent success as a soldier made all of the misery worth it, despite the fact that it kept her in the public eye. For ten years, her Feed grew from a few thousand casually curious Citizens who were curious if the General's kid could live up to his legacy, to nearly half the nation who felt she had far surpassed it. Multiple wins on Next Top Soldier and then becoming the first active-service soldier to be inducted into the MilSec Hall of Fame justified her wretched path to the top. Fame irritated her, but rubbing her success in the face of her detractors somehow made it all worth it.

Then the "incident" occurred.

Thanks to an inept lawyer, a court-martial, missing evidence, and a tribunal that seemed utterly dismissive of what the most decorated and respected soldier in MilSec history had to say for herself, that high had come crashing down around her, as if it was fated. And now she found herself in a car with traitors, on the run from the service she'd spent the last ten years of her life working for -- a life that was now ruined.

However, she had to admit, the break from the chaos of watching her entire life erode around her -- yet again -- was nice. And despite the insanity of the past day of being carted around her hometown of Atlanta in shackles by various groups in various vehicles, and the weeks of courtroom visits, teams of lawyers, and the months of solitary confinement in the Citadel military prison...she was actually enjoying this moment. Chaos was her normal state. She wasn't locked in a box. She was still alive. And, for better or for worse, at least things were interesting again.

A chirp from Jacobs's FeedMeter echoed through the vehicle.

"Holy... ten million..." Jacobs said from the front passenger seat. "Half of the Nation is watching us!"

"Oh for fucks' sake, blondie..." The driver said from behind the strangely camouflaged bandanna pulled over his mouth. He shook his head, and his long, dreadlocked ponytail shifted. "Quit obsessing over that shit. And besides, ten million is only a quarter of the nation, you idiot."

"Whatever," Jacobs answered. "Can you believe it? I'm...I mean, WE are famous!"

"No, *we* are not famous, and *you* aren't either," said the other MilSec soldier-turned-traitor, who was sitting next to Marlowe in the back seat. Her chin-length auburn hair spilled out from under her helmet as she lifted it from her head. She nodded toward Marlowe. "*She's* the famous one. We're just along for the ride. Don't get it twisted."

"Yeah, yeah, Angel," Jacobs answered, "Ten million people are watching us right now!"

The driver of the vehicle suddenly reached over and placed his hand on Jacobs's camera, twisted it off the harness and ripped it from his chest.

"Dude! What the fuck, Poet?!" Jacobs yelled.

"This isn't about your goddamn FeedMeter rank, man!" Poet said as he rolled the window down and tossed out the camera. It clattered and clanged as it bounced along the road. "You're not even supposed to be broadcasting right now. People are supposed to find us organically."

"But we have to get the message out," Jacobs said.

"Now's not the time," Angel shouted from the backseat.

"Oh, like it's your call?" Jacobs said. "You outranked me in MilSec, Corporal, but in this operation--"

"--In this operation, we follow the plan," Angel interjected. "Don't get ahead of yourself."

"I came up with the damn plan!" Jacobs snapped. "I know what we are doing! It's *my* plan!"

"Sure," Poet said from the driver's seat. "This was one hundred percent 'Operation: Jacobs's Idea,' wasn't it? Oh wait, except for the escape that I planned, or the overwatch that Angel provided, or the heavy artillery that Pariah chucked at the transport, or --"

"Whatever!" Jacobs said. "You specialists do your specialist crap, I get it. That's your job. Mine was to make it all happen."

"Just because you volunteered to be in the transport with the target doesn't make you the leader," Angel said as she removed her tactical gloves and stretched her fingers.

"The 'target'?" Jacobs asked. "You mean MK? The woman sitting right next to you? Who wouldn't even be here if it weren't for me? Is that the 'target' you meant?"

"Dude, you shot your Sergeant," Poet said. "Big deal."

"Yeah, it WAS a big deal!" Jacobs yelled. "I didn't see any of you raising your hands to ride in the belly of that beast!"

"You're MilSec Police!" Angel replied. "Who the hell else could have had access?"

"That's right, *I* had the access, and *I* pulled her out!" Jacobs said, pointing at himself and pounding his chest with his index finger. "I did this! Me!"

Jacobs looked at Poet, and then turned around in his seat to glare at Angel. He waited for a reply from either of his teammates. Neither offered one, apart from exasperated sighs.

"That's what I thought!" Jacobs said. "Go on, say it...tell me which of us got Marlowe out!"

"The Judge did," Angel said. "This is *his* operation. He put this together. Know your place."

The mention of The Judge froze Jacobs in his tracks. He took a breath and sat back in his seat. After a moment of sullen contemplation, he muttered "Well, we're still famous."

"Shut up, Jacobs," Poet said as he slowed for a stop signal. Realizing that he was breaking approximately thirty separate laws simply by driving the vehicle he was in, carrying the people that were in it, he abruptly changed his mind and slammed the throttle lever forward, flying through the red light.

"What the fuck did you just say to me?"

Poet pulled his mask from his face. "I said shut up," he repeated, looking over at Jacobs. "Need me to say it again? Okay fine: Shut up. Shut up, shut up. Shut. Up."

Jacobs stared at Poet for a moment, before finally saying, "Fuck you."

"Witty," Poet replied, returning his eyes to the road.

"Get a haircut, you reggae fuck."

"You wanna try cutting my dreads?" Poet said. "Be my guest."

"I could, you know," Jacobs said with a slight smile.

"Better men than you have tried. Even blonde ones."

"Oooooh, look at you! Mister 'Tough Guy From The Subs' pulling the super hard job of driving the getaway vehicle..."

Angel shook her head and rolled her eyes as she sunk into the back seat. Poet and Jacobs continued to bicker as the car rolled through the streets from Terminus Citadel through Five Points, into the neighborhoods of Old Atlanta.

Marlowe sat in frank disbelief -- not just because this group seemed incapable of collectively tying a shoe without picking a fight with one another, but also for the simple reason that she was even in the same vehicle as them. She had at least thirty questions flying through her brain. Who the hell were these people? What did they want with her? How did they pull off this elaborate rescue? But only question bubbled up from her lips.

"Does anyone have any food?"

The vehicle fell silent. Jacobs turned around in his seat. Angel jolted out of her reverie. Poet looked at Marlowe in the rear view mirror. It seemed to hit them all at that moment: they actually had the most famous -- and dangerous -- person in the nation sitting cuffed in their vehicle.

"Well?" Marlowe demanded, snapping them out of their starstruck trance.

"Um... yeah," Angel said, reaching into a pouch on the front of her vest. She pulled out a Battery bar and offered it to Marlowe.

Marlowe narrowed her eyes at Angel. She lifted her eyebrows and widened her eyes, as if to say *Really*? Angel looked confused. Marlowe extended her cuffed wrists as far as they would go toward Angel, which wasn't very far. She fluttered her fingers, then turned her palms upward. *How, idiot*?

"Oh right," Angel said, embarrassed. She peeled back the packaging on the nutrient-rich bar and started gingerly toward Marlowe's face with it.

"That part I can do myself," Marlowe said. "Just...put it in my hand."

Angel complied. Marlowe leaned forward and began devouring the bar in her cuffed hands.

"Think that'll be enough for you to bust out of your binds?" Jacobs asked.

"Hardly," Marlowe said with a mouth full of half-gnawed food bar. She chewed as quickly as possible, swallowing a little prematurely. She coughed, choking. Jacobs flung himself into the back seat, poised to save his hero. Marlowe shot him a look that caused him to swiftly slink back to the front.

"I'm fine," she said through her coughs. "I just haven't had...well, anything to eat in months. And to answer your question, no. These shackles...never seen anything like them before. Considering I can't even stand up straight, even at full strength, I don't know if I could manage enough leverage. I hope you guys have something in mind, because my hands are literally tied."

Jacobs composed himself. "Yeah, they're magnetically coded. I have the unlock codes from Terminus Citadel.

Poet's got an emulator at the safehouse. We can clone the release key once we get there."

"And where is this safehouse?" Marlowe asked.

"Atlanta Beach. Like, literally on the beach, in Jonesboro," Jacobs said, a smile of pride creeping across his face. "My aunt's old house. She left it to me when she died. It's pretty sweet, actually! Infinity pool with its own distillation evaporator, and a full bar, too! I know how much you like scotch, and I even got you some of your favorite cigars--"

"You're kidding, right?" Marlowe asked as she leaned down to eat the last bit of food from her fist.

"Nope," Jacobs replied. "Only the best for you, MK!"

"It's dead," Marlowe stated.

"Huh?"

"Your safehouse. It's dead."

"What are you talking about?"

"You're using a property that was in your family's name as a safehouse?" Marlowe asked. "After your Feed was watched by over ten million citizens? Your face -- all your faces -- are probably pinned in every MilSec soldier's HUD, unclosable. Everything about you is in their briefing.

Family history, property you own, places you visit...nothing connected to you is safe."

Angel looked at Jacobs. Jacobs looked at Poet.

"Don't look at me, mister mastermind!" Poet said. "The safehouse was your responsibility."

"It's solid!" He insisted. "The whole place is dark. I have a faraday cage and thermal insulation built into the walls. Power runs off a generator in a lead-lined, underground bunker. It's completely invisible! I rigged it myself. No one can scan us."

Marlowe scoffed. "So you have a house you inherited from your aunt, and you went and rigged it up to look like a gigantic black hole on a thermal scan? And that makes it safe?"

"What the hell does that mean?" Jacobs asked.

"It's a huge black spot in a sea of yellow and red. You might as well hang a sign out front that says 'Super Secret Safehouse' -- but that doesn't matter. They don't need to scan for it. It was your aunt's, right? As in she willed it to you?"

"Well yeah, but I transferred it to --"

"Doesn't matter. Your name's on the paper trail. It's dead. Better find somewhere else."

The vehicle was silent once again.

"Goddammit, Jacobs!" Angel yelled. She punched the headrest of the seat in front of her. "I told you!"

"JAQi," Poet said "Show me the feed from Location Alpha."

"Seriously?" Marlowe said with a chuckle. "Location Alpha...good fucking God, this is amazing -- wait a minute! You had to be blocked after being on NewsFeed. They have your face and your biometrics...how are you able to use JAQi with a blacklisted Pod?"

"It's rooted," Angel said, referring to the method of hacking equipment by completely overwriting its core operating system. "Poet's got a black market flash for his Pod. We will get one too, once we get clear of all this."

"And you two?" Marlowe asked, looking at Angel and Jacobs. "They're not tracking your Pods?"

"Jammed," Poet said, pointing to a small box wired into the dash of the car. "No data out, only in. Yours is, too."

"She doesn't need Pod-jamming though, do you, MK?" Jacobs said with a wink.

"How'd you..."

"I noticed the scar," Jacobs answered, pointing to an area on his own face just behind his jawbone. "And see? I told you, we thought of everything!"

A square patch of the vehicle's windscreen darkened, flickered, then displayed the Feed requested by Poet. It showed a normal looking house in a normal looking neighborhood.

"Switch to thermal," Poet said.

The screen changed from a video Feed to a temperature-based scan. Figures and objects in every house glowed in hues from red to yellow to orange, all radiating some sort of heat in every house except one, which was pitch black.

"See?" Jacobs said. "We're clear!"

"...Except for that mass of green two doors down on the left," Marlowe said, nodding toward the display. "The one that's three times larger than it should be."

"That's just thermal radiation from that house," Jacobs replied.

"It's moving," Marlowe said as she sunk back into her seat. "Houses don't move. That's reflected heat."

"Aw, fuck," Poet said with a groan. "They're using thermoptics."

Jacobs studied the screen. To the average eye, it wouldn't register. But Marlowe and apparently Poet had seen this sort of thing before: experimental camouflage that turned the wearer invisible to the naked eye and even blocked body heat...to a point.

"Thought of everything, huh?" Marlowe asked.

"Shit!" Jacobs said, punching the dashboard in frustration. "We've been compromised...JAQi, notify Team Raven and tell them to divert to... oh shit. Where are we going to go?"

"We'll have to go straight to HQ," Angel said.

"And where's that?" Marlowe asked.

"Indianapolis."

"The capital!?!" Marlowe said with a laugh. "This just gets better and better!"

"Not gonna happen," Poet stated. "This vehicle is pre-war. We've got maybe four hours' range, max. We'd need to stop and recharge at least twice."

"I have to hand it to you, Private First Class," Marlowe said, "You certainly masterminded one hell of a clusterfuck."

"Hey, we busted you out of a highly secured prison transport!" Jacobs responded. "We saved your ass! The least you could do is be thankful!"

"Thankful?" Marlowe asked. "All you've done is ensure that the entire country now believes without a doubt that I'm a traitor! And you put huge targets on your own heads! Hell, you were going to broadcast our entire trip to this supposed safehouse, and for what? Some FeedMeter rank?"

"Well, yeah," Jacobs replied. "It's part of the plan--"

"WHAT plan?!?" Marlowe yelled.

"The Judge's plan," Angel said from beside her.

"Who the hell is The Judge?" Marlowe asked. Before anyone could answer, she continued ranting. "It doesn't even matter. When -- not if, but WHEN -- we get caught, you can install FeedMeter to measure the Feed views for your execution! I'm sure you'll break your ten million viewer record! You won't even need me. You'll ACTUALLY be famous on your own!"

41

Jacobs slunk into his seat. He folded his arms over his chest and pouted. Angel leaned her head against the window and sighed. Marlowe shook her head and laughed.

"Well, let's not get caught, then," Poet said. "I have an idea."

"Great! An idea! That'll save us," Marlowe said. "And what do you have in mind? Drive us to the Super Bowl and put me in as quarterback? I'm sure the nation would love seeing me suit up again! I can see the headlines now: 'Aug Cheater and Traitor Marlowe Kana: Super Bowl MVP!' Let's just remind everyone why they should hate me even more."

"The EV plant," Poet replied.

Marlowe was about to reflexively retort, but caught herself. She thought for a moment. "Huh…" She said as her tension subsided. She nodded. "Yeah, that's actually a good idea. Damn, at least one of you thinks like a soldier."

"He's not even a soldier," Jacobs said. "And why the hell would we go to the water treatment facilities?"

"The evaporators throw out huge radio interference from the turbines, and the heat from the steam engines would mask thermal," Poet explained. "No one could scan for us."

"What he said," Marlowe said. "And if he's not a soldier, what is he?"

"I'm just a street rat from the Subs who has become a believer in the Sovereign," Poet answered.

Marlowe's eyes narrowed. "The Sovereign?" she asked.

"Let's just say we're a group who believes your story," Jacobs replied.

Angel looked over at Marlowe and nodded. Poet gave a thumbs up from behind the wheel.

"Fuck me," Marlowe said, shaking her head. "I *am* being rescued by my fan club."

Like a dysfunctional family on the road trip to hell, Marlowe, Poet, Jacobs, and Angel made the rest of the journey southeast to the water evaporation facilities in disgruntled silence. Jacobs stewed silently in embarrassment. Angel was carefully watching every car, drone, and pedestrian for signs that the group's cover may have been blown. Poet was focused on driving as normally as possible. And Marlowe? She was just plain tired.

She was just drifting off when a loud rumble emanated from under the vehicle -- the sound of wheels on gravel. They had arrived.

5. Off The Cuff

If habits die hard, training is damn near immortal. And Marlowe's training engaged the moment they arrived at the EV plant. As soon as Poet turned onto the long gravel access road, she went to work assessing the situation.

"Slow down," she ordered. "This is gravel. Keep the noise to a minimum. And kill the damn headlights."

Poet complied, and the vehicle slowly wound down the dark driveway through a dense grove of "beautifying" artificial pine trees that obscured the plant from street-level view. They approached a locked gate in the middle of a tall chain-link fence topped with razor wire, spanning nearly half a mile in either direction. The glow of what was left of the moon, combined with a single pole-mounted omnidirectional light, illuminated the area around the gate. A sign on the chain link entryway warned that the barrier was electrified, and that the current was sufficiently strong to turn a small stick figure man on the left side of the sign into a pile of ashes on the right. Billowing clouds of steam rose from stacks that towered above the operations complex in the distance. About a hundred yards from the gate was a small concrete shed.

Poet brought the vehicle to a full stop. Before anyone could say anything, he hopped out of the vehicle and approached the gate. Poet's entire childhood had been spent finding ways around old security systems in the Subs to "liberate" old items to sell for credits. And the older he got, the more silent and speedier he became. The group watched as he fumbled with the padlock holding the entrance fixed, waiting with bated breath for him to become a hunk of cooked meat. He pushed the gate open and returned to the vehicle.

"The sign said the fence was electrified," Jacobs said. "How'd you know it wasn't?"

"The fence is hot, but the gate can't be electrified," He replied as he entered the driver's side door. "Too risky for the utility vehicles. And besides, it's free-standing. Doesn't actually connect to the fence."

"Huh," Jacobs said. "Been here before, I take it?"

Poet replied with a shrug and a smile. He put the car in drive and pulled it through the gateway, immediately turned right, and drove across a small patch of concrete to the tree line where several rusty out-of-service utility vehicles were parked. He pulled alongside the farthest one from the gate, parked the car, and killed the engine.

"Okay, here we go," Marlowe barked. "The plant itself is covered in surveillance, but that utility shed on the east side looks promising. We don't have coms, so we're going to have to rely on signals. Everyone good with that?"

"I don't need coms...I've got this," Angel said, patting the scope of her rifle.

"Outstanding," said Marlowe. "Find high ground and provide overwatch. Poet, I'm guessing from your work on the gate that you're pretty handy with locks."

"One of my many specialties," he answered.

"Great. Once we get the all-clear, you'll find us a way in. Jacobs, you're on perimeter."

"What the..." Jacobs said in disbelief. "Who the hell put *you* in charge?"

"You did," Marlowe said, cocking her head and narrowing her eyes, "When you broke me out of the prison transport."

"I've got tactical command on this op!" Jacobs argued.

"You made a house directly tied to you our safehouse," Marlowe replied. "You suck. I'm taking over."

"How are you going to lead us?" He asked. "You're in shackles! You can't even walk without our help!"

"Well, that disqualifies me from doing the perimeter sweep, doesn't it? I guess that makes it your job." She nodded her head sideways as she said, "Get to it."

Jacobs gritted his teeth. He was beginning to understand the old adage of why you should never meet your heroes. "Fine," he said, "But I'm not doing this because you're in charge. I'm doing it because it's the smart thing to do."

"Of course," Marlowe said dismissively. "Now go do it."

Jacobs was so angry he missed the handle trying to open the car door. He was more successful on the second attempt, opening the door with a huff and slamming it shut behind him in aggravation.

"Christ...has that boy ever heard of covert ops?" Marlowe asked the group.

Poet chuckled. Angel simply opened her door, slid out of it, and stayed low as she began her search for high ground.

"Our turn," Marlowe said to Poet. "Let's find cover."

Poet nodded, and then exited, moving to the rear to help Marlowe from the car. Together they moved to an outcropping of trees a few yards ahead of the vehicle.

"Okay, so what the hell is all this?" Marlowe whispered to Poet as they laid low. "Who are you people?" She looked Poet up and down, and followed up with, "And what the hell are you wearing?"

Poet chuckled. "This?" he asked, tugging at the material on his sleeve, which was patterned in strange squares that slightly resembled faces. "I made it myself. I call it V-Dazzle. It's a digi-camo that tricks cameras into thinking there's a thousand faces...screws with facial recognition."

"Huh..." Marlowe said, taking a closer look. "Looks like a bunch of square smileys."

"Yep," Poet replied, "And it works, too. For now, anyway. And as for who we are and what we're about, The Judge will be able to explain it better than me. But basically, we're a group of patriots who believe that the United American State has lost its path. We are individuals who believe in sovereign citizenship. Hence the name, Sovereign."

"Sovereign citizenship?" Marlowe asked. "What the fuck does that mean?"

"We don't answer to Imagen, or their puppet-president Cook," Poet said. "We want to grow our own food...make our own products. Run our own lives. We want to return America to its core principles, the way the Founding Fathers intended."

"Huh..." Marlowe said. "What's it got to do with me? I'm a soldier, not a farmer. How the hell am I supposed to help you grow your own food?"

"You're a celebrity. You're highly respected by tens of millions of people. With you, they will listen to us. They will hear our message."

"So you want to use me as some figurehead for your idealistic bullshit movement? No fucking thanks. I'd rather be in prison."

"No, that's not..." Poet said. He sighed. "Look, I'm not any good at this. The Judge will explain it better when we rendezvous with him. I think it might resonate with you."

Before Marlowe could retort, Jacobs approached from behind them. He crouched down and gave a hearty thumbs up. "All clear," he said.

"Fine, let's move. Poet, you get us in that shed. Follow the tree line and loop back; approach from the South. Jacobs, cover him."

Poet adopted a low stance and sprinted to the utility shed with Jacobs watching from the tree line and Angel keeping an eye out from on high. While the evaporation plant itself was modern in every sense, the stand-alone utility building was decidedly low-tech.

There had been a tremendous investment by Imagen Corporation to modernize utilities in the United American State to accommodate for the conditions of the time. Potable water, atmosphere generation, and power required significant technological investment and security.

However, the buildings that held wrenches, hammers, spanners, and screwdrivers required only concrete walls and steel doors, safeguarded by old manual deadbolts and padlocks. After all, terrorists rarely attacked tool sheds, and there wasn't much of a market for hand-held tools in a society that didn't need them.

It took Poet longer to run to the door than to pick the two padlocks and deadbolt that secured it. The smell of ozone and old wood and shaved metal seeped from the cracked-open door as he slowly pulled it open. He slipped inside and performed a quick but thorough scouting of the small building's interior. Satisfied that it was secured, he hung his head out of the door and gave the signal to move in.

Jacobs helped Marlowe to her feet. He placed his hand on her shoulder and crouched down.

"What are you doing?!?" Marlowe asked as he leaned into her.

"It's going to be way faster if I carry you," he replied. "Hold still."

"You won't make it twenty yards," she protested, trying her best to resist being carried. It was no use. He laid her across his shoulders and strained as he attempted to stand.

"Wow, how much do you weigh?!?" He gasped as he finally struggled out of his squat.

"Don't you know it's impolite to ask a lady that question?"

"Is it impolite to ask what this lady has been eating? Because it feels like you've got two hundred pounds of lead in your belly."

"Metal muscles aren't light," said Marlowe. "And these shackles don't help much, either. Put me down. We're walking."

"Not a chance," He replied. "We've got a hundred yards of open terrain to cover, and you're slow. Trust me, I got this."

Jacobs began jogging as quickly as he could, which wasn't very fast at all. But his ego drove him step by step across the open field to the utility house. Marlowe would have been impressed if she wasn't so exasperated by the situation. She didn't like feeling helpless, and she liked actually *being* helpless even less. Still, with her head and feet bobbing across his shoulders with each stride they took, she couldn't help but laugh to herself. Thinking back to her professional football days, this was without question the slowest she'd ever covered the length of a football field.

Nearly a minute later, they reached the building. "Okay, what have we got?" Marlowe asked as soon as she and Jacobs entered the doorway.

"Three rooms, all clear," Poet responded. "No windows, no cameras, so we're blind. There are tools and equipment, and a cot in one of the back rooms. Someone sleeps here."

"Great," Marlowe said. "Not optimal...but it's what we got. We'll need to keep our eyes open. I'd prefer some camera coverage, but we can manage for now. Jacobs..."

"Huh?" He said through his gasps and wheezes.

"...Put me down?"

"Oh...yeah, sorry..." He responded, lowering her gently and placing her on her feet.

"What's our tool situation?" She asked. "Anything we can use to get these damn shackles off?"

Poet scanned the room. "There's a lot here, but I'm not sure how much of it is useful...hammers, vice grips, a shovel. Maybe we can whack them off with this?" He said, holding up a huge pipe wrench.

"Pretty sure none of that is useful," Marlowe said.

"Look there," Jacobs said through his panting. "In the corner. Looks like a torch...maybe we can cut through the cuffs?"

Jacobs shuffled over to the torch and lifted the nozzle, examining it. He twisted the regulator knob and looked puzzled as nothing happened. Poet came over and tapped on the tanks holding the oxygen and acetylene.

"Ah, yeah that's right," Jacobs said. As he reached out to open the valve on one of the tanks, he was interrupted by a noise outside.

He lifted his fist, signaling to the other soldiers to hold their positions and remain silent. The sound of tires on gravel grew louder.

Poet ducked behind the edge of the workbench. Jacobs grabbed Marlowe and shuffled her to the left side of the door to obscure her. He then took cover on the opposite side. The engine stopped running. A small clicking sound could be heard, followed by the creak of a rusty door. It slammed shut with a thud.

Boots crunched on gravel, getting louder as someone approached. Jacobs caught sight of a hammer on the workbench just beside him. He grabbed it and wielded it just above his head.

"What the..." A man's voice grunted from the other side of the door.

Silence. Then the sound of whispering.

The doorknob twisted. The door swung open. A silhouette spilled across the floor from the lights outside. No one entered.

"He's secured," Angel called in from the doorway. "We're coming in."

Jacobs lowered his hammer halfway and Poet rose from behind the workbench as an elderly man walked through the door with his hands up; the muzzle of a long-barrel rifle was being pushed into the back of his head. Angel followed behind.

"He's alone," she said. "No one else in the vicinity."

"Who are you?" Marlowe demanded as she shuffled forward from behind the door.

"I would ask you the same thing," the man replied. "Except, I know who you are. Been watching you for years. Question is, what the hell are you doing in my tool shed?"

"If you know who I am, then you know why we're here," she replied. "Now, who are you?"

"William Rudd," he said, extending his hand. "Pleasure."

Angel pushed the barrel of her rifle against the back of William's head as Jacobs and Poet both tensed.

"Stand down!" Marlowe ordered. The squad reluctantly complied.

"Nice to meet you, William," Marlowe said, attempting to keep the situation calm. She extended her shackled hands as far as they would go, which wasn't far at all. "We're fugitives from the law, and we're going to have to commandeer your tool house here."

William lowered his hand to hers and shook it. "Well, if you're gonna shoot me, I'd ask that you do it outside. I like to keep a tidy workshop."

"Let's not let it come to that. But we are going to have to secure you."

Marlowe nodded to Jacobs, who grabbed William and pushed him toward a chair. "Sit," he demanded.

"You don't gotta push, son," he answered as he took a seat. "I know how to sit in a chair, and I don't like being shot all that much."

Poet threw a roll of duct tape to Jacobs, who used it to bind William's wrists and ankles. He looped a few bands of tape around his torso to the back of the chair, and grabbed a small rag on a desk beside them to gag the old man.

"Aww man, not my snot rag," William said just before Jacobs stuffed it in his mouth.

Angel held her rifle on the old man as Jacobs went back to work trying to get the torch lit. Marlowe sighed, lamenting the fact that all of her training and life experience had come down to a moment where her freedom and survival depended on stuffing a poor old man's snot back into his mouth.

Jacobs opened the valve on one tank as far as it would go. A pungent aroma filled the air as acetylene gas hissed from the nozzle of the torch. Poet grabbed the flint striker from the side of the tanks and sparked it a few times, secretly delighting in the shimmering sparkles that poured from the sides. He handed it to Jacobs, who began trying to light the potent gas hissing from the nozzle.

Nothing.

"Come on, Jacobs," Poet said. "Can't you figure out a simple torch?"

"I'm not a damn engineer!" He snapped. "You're so smart, *you* do it!"

A muffled noise came from behind the rag tied around William's mouth. The squad looked over at the elderly maintenance man who was trying to communicate something. Marlowe nodded at Poet, who walked over to him and pulled the rag from his mouth.

"Mixture's too rich," the old man said.

"Huh?"

"They call it an oxy-acetylene torch for a reason, son. There's two tanks there. You can't just throw gas out and expect it to catch. You gotta bring the O2 up a bit."

Jacobs reached over and opened the green tank's valve. He struck the flint on the igniter. The torch began to roar as a bright yellow and red flame poured forth.

"There ya go," William said. "Now, tighten the valve on the nozzle until a tight blue flame...that's it!"

Jacobs grinned boyishly. He waved Marlowe over. As she shuffled toward him, William asked, "You don't intend to use that to cut them shackles off, do you?"

"Yeah, I am," Jacobs retorted. "Now why don't you shut up and let me work?"

"You didn't even know how to light the damn thing. I'm pretty sure you don't wanna be using it on a person like that."

"I'll be careful."

"Won't matter how careful you are, you're gonna hurt the lady."

"Enough," Jacobs said. "Poet, gag him again."

"Hold on," Marlowe said as Poet began to place the rag back in William's mouth. "What's the issue?"

"Whelp, them shackles are made of forged steel, looks like," he said. "Steel conducts heat. And they're wrapped around your arms, which are made of flesh. Flesh melts...after it burns."

The room was silent except for the sound of the torch burning, as the team considered the implications of William's comments. He decided their silence meant that they weren't quite grasping the situation, so he clarified. "You might get them bracelets off, but you'll probably take her hands and feet with 'em."

"Well, shit!" Jacobs shouted.

"Yeah, I'm not a fan of that idea," Marlowe said. "Is there anything else in this building we could use?"

"My saws are back at the job site," William said. "But if you give me an awl, a hammer, and about half a minute, I could sort you out."

"What good is banging on steel shackles with a hammer?" Jacobs asked.

"That's why I mentioned the awl, son," William said. "Wouldn't take but a few good whacks to bust out the pins holding the hinges between each set of them cuffs together."

"Huh...that could work," Marlowe said. "Jacobs?"

"On it," Jacobs said. He walked over to the workbench and considered the vast array of tools, scratching his head and biting his bottom lip.

"You don't know what an awl is, do you, boy?" William asked with a chuckle.

Jacobs whipped his head around, shouting, "Shut up, old man!"

"Have it your way..." William said with a shrug. "Good luck with your search."

Jacobs turned back to the bench and began picking up just about anything that looked to him like it could be an awl. He picked up several screwdrivers, one of which he brought to Marlowe to see if it was the same circumference as the pin that held the left shackle to the right. With a groan, he threw the overlarge tool to the ground and returned to his search.

"This is going to take forever," Marlowe said. She looked at Poet and nodded toward William. "Free him."

"I can find it!" Jacobs said from over his shoulder, tossing tools hither and yon.

"Let it go," Marlowe said as Poet cut away the tape holding William to the chair. "He's going to help us. Aren't you, William?"

"Well, it's that or sit with my own snot in my mouth," he replied. "Neither option tastes very good, but I reckon helping you is a damn sight better than having my workshop torn apart."

"We greatly appreciate it," Marlowe said as the last of William's binds were cut away. The old man stood and rubbed his chafed wrists, and made his way over to the workbench. He pulled open a drawer on the left and produced a long, thin, pointed piece of forged steel with a bulb-shaped handle at the end.

"Why didn't you just tell me it was in the drawer?" Jacobs asked with a snarl.

"You done did enough damage to my things," William said. "And I just reorganized that drawer."

"Alright, let's get this over with," Marlowe said. "Angel, cover him."

Angel lifted the barrel of her rifle and trained it on the man's head.

"I don't know why you gotta keep a gun on me," William remarked to Marlowe.

"We don't like taking chances," she answered.

"I mean, if it makes you feel better, go on ahead--"

"--It does," she interjected. "Are you going to help me or not?"

William shook his head, sighed, and waved her over to where he stood. "Put your hands right here on this vise," he ordered as she approached.

With a loud CLANG, she placed her bound wrists on top of the gigantic iron bench vise. William twirled the handle on the vise's tension screw until the jaws opened fully. The top and bottom edges of the massive cuffs just barely slid into the opening between the jaws.

"Tight fit," he said. "But I think it's gonna work. Now, lift up just a teeny bit...that's it. Don't want you to get pinched up in this here thing."

"How considerate," Marlowe said drily as William twisted the vise closed as tight as it would fit against the cuffs. He pushed Marlowe's shoulder and leaned her over as far as she could go. Reaching over her outstretched arms, he placed the tip of the awl against the small binding bolt holding the cuffs together.

"This ain't gonna give us much room to work," he said, "So don't be wigglin' around or nothing. I don't wanna hit you."

"Just get it done," she answered.

He grabbed a small sledgehammer from where it hung on the pegboard in front of the bench. He slowly traced the arc of where the hammer needed to swing, exhibiting the awkwardness of the angle. Suddenly, he reared back and swung wide, striking the base of the awl with a solid PING. And then another. And another.

PING after PING, the awl sunk deeper and deeper into the slot of the hinges as the bolt began to slide out, and then a loud KA-CHINK echoed through the workshop. The bolt bounced onto the workbench, and the chain holding the wrist cuffs to the ankle shackles clattered to the floor.

Marlowe heaved a heavy sigh of relief as William extracted the awl from the bolt hole. With a few twists of the vise, her wrists came free.

"THANK YOU!" Marlowe bellowed as she swung her arms around, gloriously stretching out her tight shoulders. The momentum of the heavy cuffs carried her arms forward, and then back, pulling the kinks from her muscles.

"Okay, now the hard part," William said. He wagged his finger back and forth between Poet and Jacobs. "You big, strong boys are gonna have to hold her up so I can get at them ankle cuffs."

"What," Angel said. "You don't think a girl can do it?"

"Not while holding that there gun at my head," William said without so much as a blink.

"Good point," she replied.

"Careful," Jacobs said to Poet. "She's a *lot* heavier than she looks."

"Well, yeah," Poet said, "Her entire muscular system is augmented. That's not light."

"See? He gets it," Marlowe said with a smirk.

"Shut up," Jacobs said, flinging Marlowe's right arm over his shoulder. Poet grabbed her left arm and positioned himself under her armpit. Together, the men hoisted Marlowe into the air. She lifted both of her legs as high as she could to reach the anvil. With a little assistance from William, her ankles landed with the same loud CLANG.

The veteran engineer followed the same procedure he had performed on her wrists, and in short order, the pin was jettisoned and the cuffs were separated. William freed Marlowe's ankles from the vise, and Jacobs and Poet lowered her back to the ground.

Marlowe bent over and stretched her back and legs, breathing a heavy sigh of relief. She was free, albeit still cuffed on each appendage by nearly ten pounds each of banded steel. As she massaged her arms and legs, she reflected that out of everything she'd ever accomplished: Youngest NFL MVP, multiple "Next Top Soldier" wins, MilSec Hall Of Fame inductee...no other moment from her twenty-nine years of life could compare. This was undoubtedly the best feeling she'd ever experienced.

She stood straight, rolled her shoulders a few times, and sighed. She unzipped the prison jumpsuit and pulled each of her arms out of the sleeves; the cuffs on each wrist barely sliding through the baggy fabric. She tied the sleeves around her waist and straightened the tank top she was wearing. A welcome chill ran through her as the frigid winter air cooled her exposed arms.

"Okay," she said with authority. "If we're going to hold up here, we need eyes outside. MilSec is likely going to scour every inch of Atlanta and this place will be on their radar sooner rather than later, so we need to see them coming. There's a proximity sensor and rear-view camera on the vehicle we came in, correct?"

"Yeah," Poet said. "I think I get where you're going with this."

"Good," she replied. "Get busy scouring this place for anything we can use to rig up a makeshift surveillance system. Jacobs, you get that torch prepped, we're going to need it. Angel, secure William in the back room. And be nice about it, he's a good man."

"Wouldn't I be more useful on overwatch?" Angel asked.

"You're on overwatch of our prisoner, who represents a far greater risk than an enemy we can hear coming. And we're short on time, don't waste any of it questioning my orders, got me? Now all of you -- move. Let's go!"

They all nodded and set about their tasks. Marlowe grabbed the car keys from the workbench where Poet left them and exited the building, softly closing the heavy steel door behind her. She scanned the grounds and found the opened padlocks that Poet had picked. She placed them in each of the latch hooks and locked them with a satisfying click.

Confused voices rang out as the team inside began banging on the door. Marlowe casually strolled over to the maintenance truck that William had driven up in, reached inside, and put the vehicle in neutral. It was far more difficult than it should have been for her to get it rolling, but eventually she was able to push the truck up so that the front bumper rested against the door. She kicked a small mound of gravel into a heap behind the front left tire, then reached in and pulled up the emergency brake, fixing the truck in place in front of the building.

With a smile and a light toss-and-catch of the car keys, she began jogging to the car she was brought in.

6. A Day In The Life Of: Omar Rodriguez

"Dammit, what do you WANT?!?" Omar yelled. His bark of frustration echoed in the emptiness of his apartment, directed at no one and the whole world at once.

It had been a hard day -- the hardest since he had transferred to his new civic service position at the cafeteria. People could be rude when they were hungry, and they could be especially rude when the food they ordered didn't come out just right. Not that it was Omar's fault, he was just a server. But he tended to bear the brunt of the customers' hunger-induced vitriol. He had scored much higher than a food service level on the aptitude test, but only needed a few more credits than Basic Citizen Income provided, and he didn't particularly enjoy taking classes. Plus, only a crazy person or an Aug would voluntarily join MilSec, especially Foreign Service, which was mostly staffed with felons looking to clear their records. So, even though it had its annoyances, this position was better than trying too hard...and it was certainly a step up from janitorial.

All he wanted to do now was relax, which meant chasing a few drinks with a few more drinks and then jerking off before going to sleep. He'd accomplished the first half of his to-do list, but the second kept being interrupted by pings from his friends across the net. Did the "Do Not Disturb" icon really mean nothing to them? It was mandatory at work, and he'd gotten in the habit of leaving it on during his walk home from the job -- partially to decompress and partially out of sheer laziness. His friends knew this, so they ignored the warnings and pinged him anyway. It was annoying. But in all fairness, he was guilty of the same when he really wanted their attention. And at that moment, with his hand wrapped around his rapidly declining boner, Gabby really wanted his attention.

He tucked himself away and answered the call.

"Yes?" He said as she came into view on the stand-alone screen in front of his dilapidated couch.

"Are you okay?" Gabby queried.

"I'm fine, why?"

"Well, I called like five times..."

"I was just getting home from work," he replied. "I needed a minute...sorry I didn't answer. What's up?"

"You get off at nine-thirty...it's like ten-twenty now. And you're only, like, three stops away--"

"Gabby, It's been a hard day, baby," Omar said with a sigh.

"Are you...do you need to talk?" she asked pensively.

"No, no...just a hard day, okay? What's going on?"

She looked at him with soft eyes and a face full of concern. "Well, if you need to talk, I'm here..."

"I know, honey," Omar said with a sigh.

Gabby's tone brightened forcibly. "Sooooo, have you seen NewsFeed?"

"No? I mean, not since I got home," he answered. "I know there was some craziness with MK's trial and all that. Everyone's been talking about it."

Just then, another ping appeared from John, his best friend. He'd already pinged three times according to the missed call count, which showed forty-five missed pings. "Hold on, Gabs," Omar said, flipping over to John's channel.

"DUDE!" John said. "Please tell me you are watching Cook's address right now!"

"No, I'm talking with Gabby," he said.

"You didn't get the alerts?" John asked. "Wait, I guess not, you're on DND...dude, you missed it!"

"What?"

"Corta's back!" John replied.

"What?!" Omar said. He gestured and turned the connected world back on. He saw that he'd missed a dozen news alerts, and a dozen more messages and call requests from his friends in the fantasy "Top Soldier" league he belonged to.

"Dude, this changes everything!" He exclaimed. "Gimme a minute...I'll call you back." He flicked his wrist and the call ended. Gabby reappeared on the screen.

"Hey babe, that was John. He just told me what's up. I'm gonna catch up and call you back, okay?"

"Uh...okay?" Gabby said. "Are you sure you're all right?"

"I'm fine, I swear...just give me a few?"

"Okay," she said. "I love--"

Omar ended the call and immediately began checking the notifications that he missed. "JAQi," he said, "Play the CookTalk."

"Absolutely," JAQi responded. "The entire address, or just the highlights?"

"Highlights."

"By popularity? Or chronological?"

"Whatever...just play it, okay?"

A tone sounded through the room. President Cook appeared on the screen, standing in the center of a very large stage that was lit by a single spotlight.

"...You've all been asking, and the fine people at Imagen Corporation listened," President Cook said to his audience. Twenty thousand lucky citizens who had won the audience lottery began clapping enthusiastically. Every CookTalk the President gave came with a level of excitement and anticipation unmatched by any other event, save Marlowe Kana's active duty Feed. And given the events of the day, the nation was a pot nearly boiling over with expectation.

Except for Omar. Omar was tired. He had wanted to come home, jerk off, and go to sleep. But even he had to admit, any time the President said that he or Imagen had listened to the people of the United American State, something amazing was bound to follow.

"We have been working hard on providing you with the best environments possible. Temperate summers. Lovely autumn breezes. Spring showers. And today, I am thrilled to announce a major breakthrough."

A massive screen lit up behind him. Fading into view was a scene of the capital city of Indianapolis with the capitol building front and center, encircled by administrative buildings. White particles were falling all around and collecting on the rooftops of the buildings.

"Snow."

The audience burst into astonished applause and cheers.

"Huh, that's pretty cool..." Omar murmured. "I wonder when that starts? And will we get it here in Atlanta?"

JAQi reacted to Omar's questions. The footage skipped from the raucous audience reaction to President Cook's listing of cities that would first receive snow. "--Snow will be available in all seventeen major cities in the United American State, and I am pleased to tell you that it will begin falling this evening."

The room exploded into applause yet again.

"But don't go outside looking for it just yet!" Cook said with a chuckle. "I have a few more wonderful things to tell you. For instance, not only will we be introducing snow, but we've also been able to replicate lightning and thunder. That's right, this spring, you will be able to witness actual thunderstorms."

More cheering from the crowd prompted President Cook to smile exuberantly.

"Oooooh, louder rain. Boring," Omar said. "Skip ahead."

The footage jumped to the next announcement.

"For the first time since the Reformation, atmosphere generators have gone online west of the Mississippi River. Expansion of residences westward will begin in a few months, and the applications to settle in these new territories will be accepted starting in July. My fellow United Americans, I am pleased to announce the new cities of Minneapolis, Saint Paul, and Saint Louis." Applause filled the room, and a lot of oohing and ahhing could be heard as the plans and projections for the two new cities appeared on the massive screen behind the President. "As some of the more keen-eyed have noticed, we've updated the United American State flag with the fourteenth and fifteenth stars. All digital representations have been updated, and the physical cloth flags will begin being mailed to citizens in the coming--"

"Whatever," Omar said. "It's not like I can afford to move anytime soon anyway. JAQi, skip to the Corta announcement."

The footage skipped ahead fifteen minutes. President Cook was gesturing to the right of the stage. Photos of two men in full MilSec dress blues appeared on the massive screen behind him, their names displayed below them: Alexis "Hax" Curtis and Henry "Mad Dog" Cain. A digital banner waved above them bearing the United America's

Next Top Soldier logo. A woman appeared stage-right and strode in the direction of the President, also clad in full MilSec dress uniform. The audience was on their feet, cheering and whistling and clapping. The silhouette of hands and heads partially blocked the view.

"Citizens, I give you Sergeant Sabrina Corta," Cook said as he took one step to the side and allowed the fully healed Sergeant to take center stage with him. Behind them, the pictures of Cain and Curtis separated, and a third photo appeared between them -- that of the Sergeant in full MilSec dress, her name displayed under her photo like the others: Sabrina "Senche" Corta.

The crowd lost its collective mind. Cheering and applause continued to roll despite the awkward looks exchanged between Corta and President Cook. Eventually the commotion subsided enough for the President to begin speaking again.

"Sergeant -- or can I call you Sabrina?" He asked.

"Sabrina is fine, sir," she replied stiffly.

"Well, Sabrina, how are you feeling?"

"I feel like United America's Next Top Soldier," she answered.

Every attendee leapt to their feet, and the entire room erupted in even more raucous applause and cheers.

"Ok, JAQi, got it," Omar said. The din of the cheering audience was silenced as the playback of the footage froze. "Ping John."

A tone sounded, and John appeared on the screen. "Sup?" He asked.

"Dude...Corta!" Omar yelped.

"I know, right?!"

"Okay, so what are the rules for the fantasy league?" Omar asked. "Does it work like football? Can I just bring her off injured reserve?"

"It happens automatically," John explained as he bit into an Imagen RealCheez snack chip. "You don't have to worry about that. Just make sure she's in the lineup for the next operation and you're good to go."

"Okay, got it. What is the next op?"

"Dude, you didn't watch the address?"

"Just the highlights."

"The next operation is MK," John answered. "That's it. The rules changed. No more contests or head-to-heads. It's winner takes all. Whoever gets MK wins."

"Whoa," Omar said. "Maybe I should go back and watch that then..."

"Nah, it's just a bunch of bullshit about snow and weather and stuff. They're pushing an update to JAQi tonight, but who cares. Corta and the new rules for NTS were really the only part that mattered."

"Cool," Omar said, "Thanks for the rundown. I gotta ping Gabby real quick."

"Heh, that's still a thing?" John asked, lifting the bag of chips to his lips and dumping the dusty remains into his mouth.

"Dude, come on..."

John chewed voraciously through the chip debris. "I don't get it man," he said, lips smacking. "But hey, you love her, so whatever..."

"I gotta go," Omar said.

"Later!" John said, his face blinking from existence on the screen.

"Ping Gabby," Omar asked of JAQi, who immediately complied.

"Hey," Gabby responded within a second of the notification appearing on her screen. "What's up? Everything ok?"

"Yeah," Omar said. "Caught up on the address. There's going to be snow? That's pretty crazy."

"It's going to be so beautiful!" She replied. "I'm watching out the window to see it when it starts! You want to come over and watch it with me?"

"Honey," Omar said, "I'm super tired. Today's shift nearly killed me. I'm going to crash here in a minute."

"But...it's the first ever snow in our lifetimes! In, like, five lifetimes!"

"I know," Omar said, "But there'll be more. Right now, I just wanna get some sleep."

Gabby blinked a few times and shook her head slightly. Her disappointment was clear. "Omar," she said. "We really need to...I have some things I want to discuss with you..."

"Can we talk about it tomorrow?" Omar said, exasperated. "I'm really not in a place tonight to do anything besides fall into my bed. Hit me up first thing tomorrow, okay? We can talk about whatever's going on then."

"But..."

"I love you," Omar said rigidly, much in the same way he instructed customers to have a nice day at the cafeteria.

"I...I love you too," Gabby said reluctantly. Just as she was inhaling to start her next sentence, Omar interjected with a hasty, "good night, sweet dreams!" and dropped the call.

"JAQi," he said after a short sigh. "Find some porn with actresses that look like Corta."

A tone sounded. "There are 18,422 videos with actresses that have facial features resembling Sergeant Corta," JAQi said.

"Well, fire it up!" Omar said, pulling himself back out of his pants and resuming his evening's plans.

7. Into The Subs

It was barely past midnight when Marlowe stumbled up to a doorway in a subterranean portion of Atlanta that could only be loosely considered a neighborhood. There simply wasn't a way to describe the shelters built in and around a conjoined series of damp tunnels that once were used to carry sewage. Before the atmosphere generators and the evaporators, before the biowaste separators and in-house composting, these tunnels had carried wastewater. But that was many years ago, in a time when waste being carried away by the single most precious resource on the planet wasn't considered a waste in and of itself.

Now, the sewers of Atlanta had become the Subs -- subterranean dwellings and businesses for people who didn't want to bother with the surface society above. It started as a third attempt to resurrect Underground Atlanta as a tourist destination, but it quickly became a modern day red-light district. And as more people moved down and set up shop, it expanded into the old tunnels and unused sewers that spanned old downtown. The laws in the Subs were made and enforced by the people who chose to be there. So long as whatever troubles arose in the Subs stayed in the Subs, MilSec (and the populace it protected) turned a blind eye to anything that went on.

This fact had always been very convenient for Marlowe, given her need for both back-channel information and AMP. And she could use a huge dose of both right about now.

With what little energy she had left after ditching the car in an Imagen Foods parking lot and surreptitiously hoofing it nearly two miles into the city, she rose her fist and banged on the door in front of her. And again. And again.

Marlowe lifted her head and stared up into the lens of a camera pointed down from the top of the doorway. "Come on, Jen..." she said weakly.

Finally, a rattle was heard, then the sliding of metal against metal. The door slowly creaked open. Marlowe pushed her way through it.

"Come in, won't you?" Jen asked sarcastically as Marlowe passed by.

Marlowe stumbled over to a couch made from old shipping pallets and bundles of blankets, where she then collapsed. Several of the wooden slats beneath her body groaned in disapproval. One snapped clean through in outright rebellion.

The drastically oversized sweatshirt Jen wore swayed around her like a bell as she shoved the heavy steel door shut. She felt a slight rush of air against the shorn sides of her scalp as it closed. Flinging her hand out, she slapped the switch that locked the top and bottom deadbolts in place. A hollow CLANG echoed through the room, bouncing off of the musty concrete walls of the old sewer maintenance room that Jen had turned into her home.

"Jesus, Marlowe," Jen said in exasperation, pushing a few strands of her coppery hair out of her eyes. "What the hell happened? What are you doing here? How the hell did you even escape? And who the hell were those people who broke you out?!"

"I'm fine, thanks for asking," Marlowe said. She sighed, and closed her eyes. "That's a lie...I'm not okay, Jen."

"No shit," Jen replied. "I guess that makes *me* not okay by association."

Marlowe shot a look at Jen that was both incredulous and disapproving. "I wasn't followed," Marlowe replied. "You know I'm better than that."

"Yeah, well, in your state, I'm not really ready to trust that," Jen replied. She reached out and slapped another button near the door. The lights dimmed inside and several pre-programmed scripts began running background processes to search any and all Feeds for any sign that Marlowe had been spotted. And more importantly, that she hadn't been followed. After a few anxious seconds, nothing appeared in the alert box on the screen on her desk, nor on the heads-up display in her contacts.

Jen breathed a small sigh of relief. "Nice bracelets, by the way," she said. "They totally suit you."

"Well, I was so envious of the ones *you* seem to like wearing so much," Marlowe snapped back. "I thought I'd get some for myself. Do you like--"

"--You can't stay here," Jen interjected desperately. She closed her eyes and hoped that had sounded the way she'd rehearsed a few hundred times in her head the past few weeks after witnessing Marlowe's steady downfall. However, the poker face she'd practiced for nearly all of her twenty-three years couldn't hide her pain. Maybe from other people, but not from Marlowe.

"I don't want to stay here," Marlowe replied after a moment. "I'm not looking to disrupt your new little domestic situation. In fact, I'll go as soon as I get some food and some AMP."

"AMP? What makes you think I still have that crap?"

"Because you got busted selling it a few months ago, right before my life went to shit," Marlowe retorted. "And you were released because the evidence suddenly went missing. Who do you think misplaced it?"

Jen clenched her teeth. "I got off because my lawyer--"

"--Is an imbecile who you're sleeping with," Marlowe interjected. "All he did was push some papers around. I made sure there weren't that many to push. I've never not had your back."

"Well I'm sure helping me had some benefits for you as well," Jen replied. "All that AMP that mysteriously disappeared was put to good use, I hope."

"Sure," Marlowe said, rolling her head back and closing her eyes. "Saving the world, being the hero...all that shit."

"And trying to kill one of the 'Next Top Soldier' contestants, and breaking out of prison..." Jen replied.

Marlowe sat up with a surge of fury. "How dare you!"

"What, you're automatically innocent because 'I'm supposed to know you better than that?" Jen said. "All I know about you these days is you got all famous and disappeared!"

"Fuck fame!" Marlowe snapped. "You think I care what a bunch of Feed junkies think? You think I give a rat's ass about whatever 'fame' I've gotten from a bunch of people who would just as happily watch me *die* as see me kill people, lift weights, or shop for groceries all day?"

"You certainly don't shy away from it, miss three-time Top Soldier..."

Marlowe rolled her eyes. "Whatever," she said, slumping on the makeshift couch. "Look, I can't help it if 'war' is everyone's favorite show! I'm MilSec. I have to broadcast twenty-four seven. It's the law. People watched me as I did my damn job. I kill terrorists and--"

"--keep this country safe, yeah, I know," Jen finished. "I read the bio on the back of the packaging for your action figures."

"...Fuck you," Marlowe said with a huff.

"I really like the shopping one best," she said, driving the knife in a little deeper. "Looks so realistic."

"I don't have any say in what Imagen uses my likeness for, okay?"

"No say on your own action figures, no say on product placement, no say on broadcasting on the Feeds...man, you're such a victim of the Imagen industrial complex!"

"Hey, at least I know who I am! What's your name now? 'Jen Kujaku?' Dad's silly nickname for us is your new super-secret identity? Does your lawyer fuckbuddy even know who you really are?"

"HA!" Jen chortled. "You know who you are?!? You just said you have no say in how you live your life or how everyone sees you!"

"...Just shut up and get me some food, okay?" Marlowe said.

"I bet you didn't have a say in trying to murder your competition either --"

"--Enough!" Marlowe yelled, leaping to her feet. "You know what? Fine. You don't want to help me, I'll figure it out on my own. I'm out of--"

"--Jen?" A man's voice said from the hallway. "Is everything okay?"

Marlowe and Jen both turned their heads to face a fit, balding middle-aged man clad only in his undershorts, who had appeared from the darkness of the hallway. "Wha...holy shit!" the man said as he looked at Marlowe. He turned toward Jen. "What the fuck is your sister doing here?!?"

"Michael--" Jen began to explain.

"--Adopted sister," Marlowe interjected. "And don't worry, I'm not staying."

"You're goddamn right you're not," Michael replied. "Jen, you're on probation! What the hell are you thinking? She can't be here! This is aiding and abetting a known traitor!"

"I'm not aiding or abetting," Jen said. "She just...showed up. I had to let her in."

"You had to let her in?" Michael exclaimed. "You have all these fancy locks and surveillance equipment, and you had to let her in?"

"Michael..." Jen replied.

"I'm calling MilSec," Michael stated, turning to march back to the bedroom.

"Do that and I'll have your other other testicle," Marlowe said as she sat back down.

Michael stopped dead in his tracks. "How...how do you..."

"Hoverskate accident when you were thirteen," Marlowe replied. "You had surgery. It's all on record. Well, sealed record. But hey, being me has its advantages."

Michael stammered. Jen attempted to cover her smirk. Marlowe continued. "I'm the United American State's best soldier for a reason, Michael," Marlowe said in a mocking, nasal tone. "I'm very thorough. I do my research. Especially on the lawyers who represent my sister. And double especially on the ones who she decides to let inside her."

"Hey!" Jen yelled.

"Just saying," Marlowe said innocently.

"...This is bullshit," Michael snapped. He took a step toward the doorway.

In a fraction of a second, Marlowe shot up from the makeshift couch and seized a steak knife that had been left on a plate on the table in front of her. She grasped it by the hilt, flipped it one hundred and eighty degrees into the air, and caught it by the tip. With a slight flick of her wrist, she flung the knife toward Michael, pinning the left leg of his boxer shorts to the door frame, mere inches from his remaining testicle.

Michael froze.

Jen rushed over to him. "Are you okay?" She asked, stifling a laugh.

"This is funny to you?!?" Michael asked.

"I mean...yeah? A little?" Jen replied.

"She could have cut off my...you know!" Michael exclaimed.

"It wasn't an accident. I chose not to," Marlowe said from behind them.

"Look, I'm going to get her what she needs, and then she's going to go, okay?" Jen said to reassure Michael.

"Jen, if you get caught...if they find her here...you're done. They'll execute you. And I'll be disbarred. If I'm lucky!"

Jen placed her hands on Michael's shoulders. "That's why we'll make sure they won't, okay?"

"I'll be out of your hair in no time," Marlowe replied. "Both the top hairs and the ones I just shaved."

Michael looked past Jen at Marlowe. He scowled. He returned his glance to Jen. "This is bad, Jen," he said.

"I know," Jen replied. "But she's my sister."

Michael closed his eyes and shook his head. "She is going to get us both killed."

"Michael...trust me," Jen said.

He gritted his teeth and then sighed. "You have ten minutes," he said to Marlowe over Jen's shoulder. He turned to exit the room.

"Uh, no," Marlowe said. "You're staying right here."

Michael began to retort. Marlowe reached for the fork from the same plate the knife had previously rested on.

Michael quickly shut his mouth and took a seat in the makeshift chair near the couch.

"Good boy."

"Leave him alone," Jen said. "I'll go get your shit, but then you need to go."

Marlowe lifted her hand and lazily waved Jen off. She turned and disappeared down the hallway.

Marlowe stretched her arms over her head, then interlaced her fingers and rested her palms on the back of her skull as she sighed. Michael sat with his hands in his lap, visibly uncomfortable.

The screen on Jen's desk continued the nearly endless recapping of the events that had transpired in the past twenty-four hours. Everything from the footage of Marlowe attacking Sergeant Corta in the locker rooms of their barracks, to Marlowe's guilty verdict at the trial, to the sentencing hearing, to the prison break and the subsequent sniping of the camera drones by the soldiers who had sprung her -- everything was being covered and analyzed in frenzied, minute detail. Various recap blurbs crawled across the bottom of the screen while the NewsFeed anchors bantered with assorted experts in fields from legal, to MilSec domestic operations, to psychology.

Marlowe was glad the audio was muted. She never could stand her own press. Still, she couldn't help but keep one eye on the footage. Suddenly, NewsFeed cycled through something Marlowe wasn't familiar with: a recap of the announcements by President Cook regarding "Next Top Soldier" and the return of Sergeant Corta. And the fact that capturing Marlowe was now the sole determination for victory.

Marlowe sat up straight. The entire nation may have been glued to their screens for the better part of three months, but she was watching all of this for the first time. Seeing Corta standing beside President Cook alive and well was genuinely intriguing.

"JAQi, turn up the volume," she said aloud.

There was no response.

"JAQi..." Marlowe grimaced. "Ah, fuck, I keep forgetting..." she said, shutting her eyes.

"They flashed your Pod, right? When you were arrested and processed?" Michael asked.

Marlowe looked over toward Michael. She was too exhausted at this point to be a smartass. She simply nodded.
"Huh... The Prisoner Operating System has GPS. How did they not track you during the escape?"

"They can't," Marlowe answered. "I performed a little...self-surgery when I was inside." She tilted her head and pointed to a small scar behind her left ear, just above her jawbone. "No Pod, no POS."

"Christ!" Michael said, wincing. "That couldn't have felt good."

Marlowe answered by raising her eyebrows and shrugging. With a sigh, she laid her head back and closed her eyes once more.

"Well, it wouldn't work here anyway," Michael replied. "Jen keeps things dark. No JAQi here. No outside connections. All closed feeds and proxied connections."

"Yeah, I forgot about that, too," Marlowe replied. "It's...been a while."

"So I understand." Michael replied. "You two used to be close, right?"

Marlowe sighed as she leaned forward and looked at Michael. "Look, she likes you. I'm happy for you both. And I get that you get off on taking charity cases and playing the role of savior. But I don't need a therapist. I don't need you to save me. I just need to get my shit and figure out how to clear my name."

"I may not be a therapist," Michael said, leaning forward, "but I'm a damn good lawyer. Let me help you. I will--"

"--You'll what? Get the MilSec tribunal to overturn a guilty verdict for treason? For a soldier who was seen on the national NewsFeed being sprung from a prison transport by domestic terrorists?"

"Yes!" he replied. "You'll turn state's evidence. Testify against the MilSec soldiers who illegally kidnapped you and name the terrorists who assisted them. Tell the tribunal you had nothing to do with--"

"--That didn't work at my first trial," Marlowe interjected. "They still found me guilty of treason, despite conclusive evidence that I acted in self defense against Corta and her little clique. They suppressed the footage. I doubt they even covered that on NewsFeed, did they?"

Michael looked at her, puzzled. "No?"

"Yeah, well...fat chance they'd believe me now," Marlowe said. "Or even care if they did."

"The way I see it, you really don't have any other choice," Michael replied.

"Sure I do," Marlowe said. "I can clear my name. Or die trying."

"And get us killed in the process..." Michael muttered.

"I'll be gone long before anyone even thinks to look for me here...if they even know to look here," Marlowe answered. "I just need--"

Jen emerged from the hallway clutching a green duffel bag.

"--That," Marlowe continued.

Jen tossed the bag into Marlowe's lap. Marlowe unzipped it and let out a massive sigh of relief. In it was several stacks of perfectly legal Battery energy bars, along with a dozen or so exceedingly illegal inhalers loaded with AMP.

Michael's jaw dropped. "Is that AMP?" Michael asked Jen.

"Yup," Marlowe answered for her. She immediately ripped open the packaging on a Battery bar and began devouring it.

"Jennifer! How could you?!?" Michael asked.

Jen ducked her head and sighed.

"Your girlfriend's a drug dealer," Marlowe said while chewing on the last bit of the extremely calorie-dense energy bar. "And a card shark, and a thief, and a really good hacker. But yes, among those other things, she deals drugs. And these are drugs...well, not this," she said, a crumb falling from her mouth as she waved half a Battery bar at him.

Michael narrowed his eyes, clearly unamused.

"But these..." Marlowe grabbed an AMP inhaler, placed it in her mouth, pressed the blue button on the top, and took a deep breath. After a moment, she exhaled. She shivered and shook from head to toe. "Oh, yeah...THESE are drugs. Good ones, too. I mean, real grade-A stuff. Better than your average street shit."

Michael sat in his seat, stunned and hurt. Marlowe began unwrapping a second Battery bar. "Huh," she said, noticing the wrapper. "They took my picture off the package."

"Of course they did," Jen said. "They're not going to let a criminal represent their product. And you should slow down. You're going to puke."

"Fine, at least I'll puke actual food," Marlowe replied. "Do you know how long it's been since I've eaten anything other than vitamin supplements and water?"

"Three months, five days, and a few hours," Jen replied.

"...Sure. Something like that."

"Well, even *your* science experiment of a body can't absorb that much nutrition that quickly," Jen said.

"Okay, well, if I waste it, I waste it," Marlowe replied. "It's not like you care. You wanted me out of here. I'm out of here."

Marlowe stood to leave. Her head spun and she immediately fell back on the makeshift couch. This time it couldn't hold her immense weight. The entire structure collapsed beneath her.

"Shit...Marlowe..." Jen said, exasperated. She went over to help Marlowe up.

"I'm fine..." Marlowe said, pushing Jen's hands away.

"Clearly. Take my damn hand."

Marlowe reached out and grabbed Jen's hand. Jen groaned as she strained to hoist Marlowe up. Woozily, she leaned on Jen, who guided her to the empty seat next to the collapsed couch.

"You think I did it, don't you?" Marlowe asked.

"I think you're in a world of trouble," Jen replied softly. "And I think your options are pretty limited. In fact, I think you're severely fucked."

"You didn't answer my question," Marlowe stated. "I am telling you right here and right now, I am innocent. I was attacked first and was defending myself. I want to hear you say you believe me."

Jen placed her face in her palms.

"Jen!" Marlowe barked.

Jen sighed. She lifted her head and looked at Marlowe. "Look, you say you didn't do it, and I believe you," she said. "You say there's evidence that proves you're innocent, and I believe you. But Marlowe...it doesn't matter what *I* believe! You were found guilty of treason. You were sentenced to life in prison. You escaped and are now considered a traitor and a fugitive."

Marlowe looked up at Jen, who could detect a note of vulnerability somewhere in her eyes.

"You're literally the most recognizable face in the nation. Short of getting a complete face replacement, I don't think you have any options left. Let us help you. I know some MilSec people, guys who buy from me. They'll listen to you."

"We can fight this," Michael said, emerging from the kitchen holding a bottle of scotch in one hand and a small box of cigars in the other.

Marlowe did a double-take. She hadn't noticed that Michael had left the room, much less that she had been sitting in the seat he had vacated.

"I have a plan...if you'll hear me out," he said, offering Marlowe the bottle and the box.

Marlowe considered him for a moment. His existence on this planet was appalling to her. He embodied everything she hated about the society she spent her adult life protecting. The product of wealth and entitlement, the scumbag lawyer before her skated through life on the mistakes of others. And now he was slumming with Jen, spending his nights playing tourist in the Subs amongst the people he spent his days milking credits from, defending them against minor charges that usually had no merit to begin with and were easily dismissable.

But then again, he had scotch, cigars, and a plan -- three things she'd not had in months. She reached out and took his offerings.

"First, I want to know what happened," Michael said, taking a seat on the edge of the table, barely missing the plate with the fork. "Tell me everything. I'll believe you. I can help you."

Marlowe popped the cork on the bottle and took a long swig. She let out a massive sigh. It didn't matter that it was cheap synthetic stuff, or that Scotland no longer existed. It said "Scotch" on the bottle and right then, it was the best thing she'd ever tasted.

"Well," she said, cracking the lid on the box of extremely rare, vintage Cuestas cigars and removing a stogie. "You already know the back half of it...the footage of me tossing Corta around the barracks and nearly killing her. All that."

She removed the cigar from the wrapper, placed it to her nose and inhaled deeply. It was real. How this two-bit lawyer came across a box of Cuestas didn't matter to her, nor did the fact that it was a little stale. At that moment, it was pure heaven. She used the guillotine cutter she found in the box and lopped off a small sliver from the head of the cigar.

"What you don't know is that she attacked me first."

"So you said in your testimony," Michael replied. "But there's no evidence. And believe me, Jen tried to find it."

"I called in every favor I had," Jen said. "Scraped every Feed, chased down every lead. There's absolutely nothing out there that backs up your story."

"Yes there is," Marlowe replied as she placed the cigar in her mouth. She pulled a match from a box and struck it. Even the sulfur smell of the matchstick igniting brought a smile to her face. "It was suppressed. But it does exist."

She placed the match to the foot of the cigar and inhaled deeply, puffing continuously to get it to ignite. Cherry-red embers glowed at the foot of the cigar. Marlowe took a deep drag, held the smoke in her mouth, and exhaled. She would have shed a tear, if her ocular implants hadn't made that impossible.

"Where?" Michael asked, snapping Marlowe back to the present moment.

"It was some private," Marlowe replied. "His Feed was broadcasting. It picked up Corta's ambush in the shower."

Suddenly, the security script that Jen was running sounded a loud DING, followed by another.

Jen snapped to attention. "Fuck," she said under her breath as she leapt toward the terminal on her desk. Marlowe followed suit with Michael close behind.

Two windows on the desktop screen showed footage that matched the search script's parameters. One was displaying a MilSecFeed from Sergeant Henry Cain, with statistics that showed nearly ten million citizens were watching it live. The other was the exact same feed, simulcast on NewsFeed, indicating that nearly three-fourths of the nation was tuned in.

"Breaking News: 'Next Top Soldier' contestant Henry "Mad Dog" Cain, tracking Marlowe Kana: Live." read the crawl under the NewsFeed footage.

"Well, look at that," Marlowe said grimly. "It's your neighborhood's front door." She whipped around to face Michael and grabbed him by the throat. "Your dipshit hack lawyer boyfriend gave them the address when he went to get my scotch."

Michael raised his hands and began pleading. "I didn't! I swear...I wouldn't..." he croaked.

"Never trust a lawyer bearing gifts," Marlowe snarled. "Especially alcoholic ones."

"Let him go, Marlowe!" Jen begged. "He didn't do anything...just...please..."

Marlowe stared directly into Michael's fear-filled eyes. With a slight smirk, she released his throat and pushed him, sending him flying backwards into the table in front of the collapsed couch. He fell backwards and landed in the debris.

Marlowe walked over toward him. She reached down. He flinched. She grabbed a slat from the broken furniture and began swinging it around testing its heft, considering its use as a weapon. "You're lucky I love my sister," Marlowe said. "I should have just killed you in the first place. My fault for being lazy. And tired. And hungry."

"Fuck! Fuck fuck fuck!" Jen screamed. She bolted for the hallway in an attempt to flee.

Marlowe caught Jen by the arm. "No chance in hell," Marlowe said. "We have to handle them. If we run now, they'll be on us like a hunter drone. And so will the hunter drones."

Jen looked into Marlowe's eyes. They were bloodshot and quivering -- effects from the AMP Marlowe had whiffed.

"They're not supposed to...shit, we're fucked!" Jen yelled.

Marlowe gritted her teeth. "No," she said with authority. "I can handle this wannabe 'Top Soldier' and his little squad."

"Well, run out there and go get them!" Jen yelled. "Go! Get out of here!"

"You know how stupid that is," Marlowe replied as she began scanning the room for weapons. "I can't fight them in the tunnels. I'll be flanked and have to fight from both sides. Better to stand our ground here."

Jen sighed. She raised her hands and her eyes glowed slightly as she moved her fingers, typing in the air, pinning the Feeds to her HUD and setting new scripts to trigger if any others began broadcasting. If she was going to wait this thing out, she needed to know exactly what was happening as it happened.

"I swear, I didn't do it!" Michael pleaded.

"Yeah, fine, whatever," Marlowe said. She checked the footage on the screen and saw that Cain and his squad had arrived. "It doesn't matter now. They're here."

8. Mad Dog Barking

Michael wrung his hands as he paced the room. "Yes...this is our only option," he announced.

"So you've said," Marlowe replied. "Several times."

"No!" Jen yelled, clutching Michael's arm. "This is insane! You can't go out there, they'll kill you!"

"They wouldn't dare," Michael scoffed. "The entire nation is watching. Besides, I am a highly regarded lawyer, and we have the law on our side."

"Jen, let him go," Marlowe said, relighting the cigar she'd let burn out. She turned her attention to Michael. "You invited them here. You wanna go say hi to your soldier buddies? Go say hi, mister 'highly regarded' lawyer."

"I didn't..." Michael began to argue before he was interrupted by an amplified voice from the other side of the door.

"This is your final warning!" The voice on the loudspeaker blared. Marlowe recognized it as the voice of Henry "Mad Dog" Cain, full of swagger and arrogance. "Come on, MK! Surrender now, and I promise, no one will get hurt."

Marlowe exhaled a puff of smoke and sneered. "I hope he's including himself in that statement."

"Huh?" Jen asked.

"He knows that even though I'm not tip-top, I can still whip his ass," Marlowe answered. "Remember season two of 'NTS'? He went against me in a head-to-head. I went to judo-throw him; I grabbed his arm and pulled." She placed the cigar to her lips and took a long draw, exhaling it through her nose. "The arm went flying, but the rest of him…anyway, that's why they took out intra-squad trials."

Jen sighed. "Marlowe, you know that I never watched…whatever. It looks like he got a new arm," She said, staring at the screen on her desk as she watched Cain's squad secure their position outside her front door. "A really big and shiny new one."

"Augs are only as good as the person they're attached to," Marlowe remarked calmly. "Even big shiny arms."

"Look," Michael said, returning to business. "Article Thirty-Seven guarantees your right to an appeal. We can find that evidence you described. You can tell them how you were kidnapped by those crazy traitors. We can win this. We have the law--"

"--on our side. Yeah," Marlowe interjected. "You've said that a few times, too."

"Michael..." Jen pleaded.

"Don't worry Jen," Marlowe interjected. "You heard the nice guy on the loudspeaker with the huge metal arm. They're not going to hurt us. He promised."

"Okay, I'm going out there," Michael said.

"Go get 'em, tiger," Marlowe said, drawing from her cigar.

Michael closed his eyes, inhaled deeply through his nostrils, and exhaled through his mouth. "Right...here goes," he said, reaching reaching up to press the switch by the door. He hesitated a moment before slapping the button. The magnetic seals buzzed as they released. He grabbed the bar securing the door and slid it back, then cracked the door open.

He peeked his head outside only to see half a dozen heavily armored soldiers, all pointing rail guns at him. Cain stood just beyond them, commanding from behind a wall of his men. Michael's forehead was immediately decorated with half a dozen red targeting dots.

"Hold your fire!" Michael yelled, raising his hands and taking a step outside to face the MilSec squadron. "I represent--"

The door slammed closed behind him. The magnetic seals buzzed.

"MARLOWE!" Jen yelled. "What are you doing?"

"Saving our lives," she replied. "Move." Marlowe pushed Jen out of the way and began dragging the desk toward the door.

Outside, Michael was sweating. His arms raised over his head and his voice creaking, he began pleading with the soldiers staring at him down the barrels of their rifles.

"I represent Marlowe Kana," he said with a cracking voice. "By the authority of the Valor Writ, I hereby evoke Article Thirty-Seven on behalf of my client. She has the right to an appeal before the tribunal--"

"FIRE!" Cain ordered.

Metal slugs whipped through the air and in less than a second, Michael was reduced to a smoking ball of bloody meat.

"Oh wow...well THAT didn't go well!" Marlowe said with a chuckle. She dragged a bookcase loaded with technical manuals and security books to the other side of the doorway, creating a makeshift tunnel. "Jen, you got your special insurance policy on this place?"

Jen stared blankly at the screen. Michael's bloody corpse was featured through the lens of Cain's Feed.

"JEN!" Marlowe yelled, grabbing her by the shoulders.

"..Wha?" Jen replied as she turned to face Marlowe, eyes wide, jaw hanging open.

"This place...it's wired up, right?" Marlowe asked.

"Uh...yeah," Jen replied.

"Okay," Marlowe said, tossing boxes on top of the desk to create cover, "I'll buy us some time. Go get everything prepped, and when I say so, hit the switch."

"You... you killed him..."

"No, THEY killed him! They murdered him in cold blood in front of the entire nation, and I'm sure the audience just loved it. Ratings for 'Next Top Soldier' are sure to skyrocket. Michael did his country a great service."

"You cold-hearted bitch!" Jen cried, emerging from her stupor. "How could you just let him go out there and face those monsters?"

"Well I didn't think they'd actually *kill* him!" Marlowe retorted as she pulled the chair she had been sitting on alongside the bookcase. "I guess the rules of engagement change when ratings are on the line!"

A loud WHAM echoed from the door. And then another.

Marlowe checked the Feed on the screen. Two soldiers manned a battering ram, while another two stood on either side of the door, preparing to breach. Cain stayed behind the formation of soldiers keeping their sights trained on the doorway.

"That coward," Marlowe said. "Fancy cybernetic arm and he can't even knock on the door himself..."

"Michael was trying to help us!" Jen yelled, tears streaming from her eyes. "He was trying to help YOU!"

Another WHAM. And then another.

"Look, now's not the time for this!" Marlowe snapped. She grabbed the green duffel bag, pulled out one of the AMP inhalers, and then held out the bag toward Jen.

"Blow the place up with me in it, or take this and yell at me when we get out of here. But either way, it's time for you to go."

Another WHAM.

Jen bit her lip and clenched her teeth. With a tearful sigh, she nodded, grabbed the bag, and turned to leave.

"Lock the door and don't open it!" Marlowe yelled. "Not for anyone, including me!"

Jen retreated down the hallway as the soldiers continued ramming the door in perfect rhythm. Marlowe sighed, emptying her lungs. She placed the inhaler to her mouth and took a second full hit of AMP. After a quick shiver, she stretched her neck and cracked her knuckles.

"Okay, Jen was right," she said, "I'm definitely going to puke."

She listened closely as she picked up the hunk of wood from the collapsed couch. Another WHAM. And then another WHAM. And then, before the ram could hit again, she tossed the chunk of couch at the switch by the door. The magnetic seals buzzed, and the door creaked open, just in time for the soldiers to come surging forward, wildly off balance.

Marlowe sprinted toward them, grabbing the head of the battering ram. She locked her feet in place, and with all the power she could muster from her recently fueled up muscles, she pulled the ram forward, yanking the soldiers into the doorframe on either side.

She retreated with the battering ram down the choke point she'd created and took cover. More soldiers filed in in two-by-two cover formation. As they spread out at the end of the furniture tunnel, Marlowe swung the ram like a bat at the soldier nearest her, cracking his helmet and knocking him out cold. She then grabbed the handles of the ram, leapt forward, and demonstrated that the head of a battering ram could punch through the chest cavity of a human being if thrust hard enough.

She reestablished cover behind the other side of the choke point at the doorway. Well-versed in MilSec tactics, she knew what was coming next. She took a very deep breath, ducked her head, closed her eyes, and plugged her ears.

Several flash grenades flew through the doorway and detonated.

Textbook, she thought to herself as more soldiers filed into the house through the tunnel choke point. One of the soldiers turned in her direction with his rifle at the ready. Marlowe grabbed the gun by the barrel and yanked as she took a step to the side, pulling the soldier off his feet and causing him to pull the trigger. The barrel seared her hands, but adrenaline and AMP kept it from registering with her nervous system.

It, however, couldn't prevent her from smelling her own cooked flesh. The stench, combined with the calorie-dense Battery nutrition bars and the first real cardio exercise she'd had in months all made her astonishingly queasy. As another soldier rounded the corner, she spewed milky white vomit on him.

"Agh!" The solder shrieked before Marlowe swung the rifle by the barrel at his head and knocked him out.

Two more soldiers came from the other side of the room after clearing their assigned corners, only to find themselves staring at a gagging, pissed off Marlowe Kana. They raised their rifles.

"Goddammit! I said no shooting!" Cain yelled as he marched through the doorway. "Who the hell fired that round?"

The two soldiers looked his way, then pointed at the puke-covered soldier at their feet.

Cain retched and said "Well, that smells just lovely."

"I got more if you want it," Marlowe said, brandishing the biometrically protected rifle by the barrel like a baseball bat. She couldn't use it to shoot, but it was far from useless. "Come and get it."

Two more soldiers filed in behind Cain and raised their rifles at Marlowe. Four red dots adorned her face.

"Good to see you again, MK!" Cain said. "Love the bracelets."

"Nice to see you too, Cain," she retorted. "Love the new arm."

He patted his augmented right arm with his natural hand. "Yeah, I suppose I have you to thank for it. But I'm not mad...I actually love it. But as much as I'm dying to show you how well it works, it'd be better for both of us if you surrender."

"And make you United America's Next Top Soldier?" Marlowe retorted. "No way in hell."

"You are outnumbered and have no place to run," Cain stated. "The prize is doubled if I bring you in alive, but I won't hesitate to order my squad to fire."

"So I saw a few minutes ago," Marlowe said drily. "Big brave 'Mad Dog' Cain...having his squad do all his dirty work. I'm sure everyone watching the Feeds right now is super impressed at how you're able to tell your squad to shoot an innocent lawyer."

Another squad of eight soldiers arrived on the scene and entered the doorway.

"Hold your positions!" Cain ordered. "I got this."

Marlowe smirked. "Ah, so there *is* some fight in you."

"You're about to find out," Cain replied. He tapped a switch on his right arm and it began to hum with electricity.

"Oh goodie," Marlowe said, dropping the rifle-turned-club. "I *do* get to see how that fancy arm works!"

Cain chuckled. He reared back and then swung at Marlowe with all his might. Marlowe took one step to the side. The entire room echoed with a loud CLANG as Cain's powered fist slammed into the steel partition wall behind her.

Marlowe raised her fist to retaliate. The squad raised their rifles and trained them on her.

"Oh, would you look at this!" Marlowe said. "The Mad Dog needs his little puppies to back him up!"

Cain growled. "Lower your weapons!" he ordered his team.

"But sir..." one of his squad members stammered.

"That's an order!" Cain demanded.

The squad complied and lowered their weapons again. Cain began to circle Marlowe. He clenched his metallic fist and raised it at her. "You're mine," he said.

"You're pathetic," she replied with fists raised. She circled to the left, maneuvering Cain between her and the soldiers that stood by, agape at what they knew was going to be a fight for the ages.

"Come on!" Cain yelled, pounding his fist on his chest. "I'll even let you take the first--"

Marlowe leapt into the air, lunging at Cain. Her right fist cocked fully back, she punched directly into the middle of his chest as she landed. Her overwhelming strength sent Cain flying backwards into his squad.

Cain's body armor absorbed the force of the blow and dissipated it across his body, keeping her fist from sinking into his chest and ripping out the other side. Cain, however, momentarily lost his breath and balance, and his squad took the brunt of his weight. Like dominoes, they fell and tossed around in all directions.

Cain's adrenaline kicked in. He rose to his feet and stumbled forward, swinging his powerful augmented fist. The weight of his massive hand hit nothing but air and sent him spinning right back to the ground with the rest of his squad, who were clambering on and around one another trying to get up.

Marlowe was already halfway down the hallway making her getaway. Without breaking her stride, she planted her left foot just above the door handle. The steel door took the the kick, and the deadbolt sheared clean away. The door slammed open so hard, the handle chipped away a sizable divot in the concrete wall.

Jen's heart skipped a beat and a light shriek escaped her lips as Marlowe burst into the room. She had just pulled back the carpet and opened the hatch to a system of drainage tunnels once meant to handle overflow rainfall...back when rain still fell.

"Gotta go!" Marlowe yelled as she slammed the door shut. She yanked the dresser next to the doorway over on its side as a makeshift barricade.

"Move!" She yelled to Jen, who had just picked up a small device from her bedside table.

Jen nodded. She grabbed the top rung of the ladder and began to descend just as Cain's powered metal fist punched a hole through the top of the barricaded door.

"GO!" Marlowe barked, placing her foot on Jen's head and kicking her down the tunnel.

Cain grabbed a side of the hole and began furiously ripping the metal door apart.

Marlowe turned and jumped down the tunnel opening, grabbing the top of the hatch as she fell. It slammed closed behind her.

"Hit it!" She said to Jen, who had just sat up trying to regain her bearings. Jen looked at her empty hand. The remote had fallen a few yards away. She lurched forward and scrambled on her hands and knees toward it.

The hatch opened just as Jen reached the detonator. She glimpsed Cain's metal fingers lifting up the hatch as she hit the button. The muffled sounds of explosions rumbled above the tunnel. The hatch fell shut. Screaming could be heard as flames danced around Cain's hand in the cracked opening of the tunnel hatch.

Marlowe reached her hand down toward Jen. Jen took it. Without a word, they fled into the darkness.

9. A Day In The Life Of: Glen Russel

Sweat poured from Glen's brow and soaked his sweatshirt. This was by far the hardest thing he'd ever done in his life: one hundred freaking push-ups in a row. With grim remorse, he recalled how he had been absolutely certain that Cain would win United America's "Next Top Soldier." He never thought that he'd have to be the one to make good on the bet. But honor was everything with "The Night Crew" at his gym. And a bet was a bet.

"Come on, Glen!" A voice called out from somewhere in front of him.

"Dude, you got this!" Another said from his left.

"Just a few more, bro," A third voice urged from his right.

Sweat dripped from his chin. He'd already powered through eighty-four push-ups. He'd never completed that many in a row before. And despite feeling a bit embarrassed that he'd picked the wrong dog in the fight, he was still proud. For one thing, he was contributing to the Grid, and that always felt great. It was one of the main points of pride in staying in shape: being able to contribute your stored kinetic motion to the United American State's power grid. Doing your part to keep the lights on. But this...this was special.

This was a personal best. And everyone loved a guy who achieved a personal best.

"Glen, don't give up!" A female voice said from somewhere nearby. Glen knew the voice. It was the voice he was secretly hoping he'd hear. Gwendolyn was there. She was cheering him on.

This was his moment. He couldn't stop now.

He pressed as hard as he could and brought his body to a plank position. "Eighty-five!" His trainer shouted. "Good job, Glen!"

Glen looked up and glimpsed the screen on the far wall of the gym. Cain's face was splashed all over it. Just as he'd caught sight of it, a huge red "X" appeared over Cain's photo.

"I told you, bro," one of the voices near him said, "Corta's winning this season!"

"I can't believe you bet on Cain, Glen!" Another voice crowed.

Glen grimaced, half from frustration that he wasn't quite able to block out the voices, and half from the unbearable fire that burned in his chest and shoulders and arms. He wanted to stop. He wanted to die. He wanted more than anything to go back in time and take back the bet he'd made earlier.

But then, Gwendolyn's gym shoes came into view. Attached to them, Gwendolyn's legs, clad in skin-tight yoga pants. And at the top of those legs, he knew, was Gwendolyn's perfect ass.

That's all he needed to see.

"Eighty-six!" His trainer yelled. "Eighty-seven...eighty-eight! YES!"

"Come on, Glen!" Gwendolyn yelled. "You can do it!"

Glen dug deep. Somewhere inside him was the remaining twelve push-ups. Through fire and pain, he found them.

"ONE HUNDRED!" His trainer yelled.

Everyone clapped and cheered as Glen collapsed into a heap on the floor.

"Now that's respect right there, bro!" a voice from somewhere behind him said.

"Way to go, Glen!" another chimed in.

"Of course he did a hundred push-ups," a withering voice said, "He's augmented."

"Dude, not cool," the first voice retorted. "That's super Aug-ist. Besides, it's just his legs that are augmented."

"Whatever," the detractor said. "You never know with these Auggies. They *say* it's just their legs, but then they get their hearts and lungs and muscles replaced and come to our gym where natural citizens are contributing to the Grid, and set all kinds of records, and, like...you never know! Just look at that traitor MK."

"MK was different," a new voice said as it entered the conversation. "I don't mean to butt in, but I couldn't help overhearing. Marlowe technically didn't break the rules. And besides, she publicly stated that she didn't know--"

"--Oh, don't give me that tired old bullshit!" the other voice scoffed. "So what, the rules may have said that you have to declare 'external augmentations' but you know as well as I do, they meant ANY augmentations! And she claims that she didn't know she had Augs until the test was modified to detect internal ones? What, you're fifteen years old and running faster and jumping higher and hitting harder than anyone else in the entire UAFL? And you're a girl? And you don't know you have Augs? Bruh...come on."

"Oh, wow, now you're an Aug-ist AND a sexist?" The other voice swiftly upgrading in tone from defensiveness to anger.

"I'm not sexist! I believe *anyone* can play, as long as they score. But seriously...a teenage girl laying out dudes three times her size like she did? And claiming to be natural? Dude..."

"But MK thought she *was* natural," the new voice said. "Everyone did. No one knew. The league couldn't test for nanofiber then."

"That's my point! They should have known based on her being a little girl, you know? Because she sure as hell knew, and she lied, man. Just like your boy here is probably lying about his Augs being only in his legs."

"You're an asshole!"

"Hey, folks," Glen's trainer piped in, "Just...move on, okay? This is Glen's moment. Go have this conversation somewhere else."

"I'm done talking to this Aug-ist shitheel anyway!"

"Fuck you, Aug-lover!"

The argument subsided as they parted ways. Still laying face down in a puddle of his own sweat, Glen could barely hear them over the sound of his own blood pumping through his eardrums. It really didn't matter what was being said. He was proud of himself. Both for achieving a new personal record, and for looking pretty badass in front of Gwendolyn. A smile crept up from deep inside and made its way onto his face.

A beep sounded from his kinetic storage device. A new personal record -- and a massive contribution to the power grid.

"I am SO proud of you, bro!" His trainer said, extending a hand to help him up. Glen rolled to his side, reached up, grasped it and let his trainer pull him to his feet.

"Wow," Gwendolyn said, smiling at him with perfect pearly white teeth. "That was super impressive."

"Thanks," Glen said through huffs and puffs. "It really meant a lot to me, you cheering me on like that."

What am I doing, thought Glen. He was so tired yet so amped up from his achievement that he'd forgotten for a moment that he was normally too much of a wimp to even exchange words with Gwendolyn. But hey, everyone has to have their moment. And he was clearly in the middle of his. He'd had a crush on Gwendolyn since the day he joined the gym. Maybe today was the perfect day to make his move. Maybe this was the moment he'd be telling their kids about in fifteen years; the moment that he finally had the courage to ask their mother out on a--

"--Gwen, you ready, babe?" A voice said from behind him.

A muscular, tattooed guy sauntered past Glen and wrapped his arms around Gwendolyn.

"Hey baby! Yeah, let's go!" Gwen said as a smile spread across her face. "I'm so glad you were able to make it to town this weekend. Oh, good job, Glen!" She waved over her shoulder as she left.

"Yeah," Glen said, waving back. "Thanks."

"Bro!" Glen's trainer said as he slapped Glen on the back. "Upload your K's and let's hit the showers!"

Glen reluctantly smiled and nodded. He removed his kinetic storage unit from the belt around his waist and connected his unit to the rack. Of course she was already taken. *Just my luck.*

Glen trudged toward the showers. He glanced up at the Feed on the gym wall to see the reporters blaring on about the latest development in the ongoing saga of Marlowe Kana. Her father, General Ashish Kana, had just been arrested and charged with treason for allegedly aiding in Marlowe's escape.

"Man," Glen's trainer said, "Can you believe this MK shit, bro?"

"It's certainly a mess," Glen said, delivering his standard line whenever current events came up at the gym.

No one could ever get mad at a reply like that. He wished he'd stuck to that policy earlier instead of making the bet. But he had been feeling ballsy. Just like when he had finally worked up the nerve to speak to Gwendolyn.

That's what bravery gets you. But then again, I just did a hundred push-ups. That's something to be proud of.

Smiling the first genuine smile he'd had since his accident, Glen made his way to the showers.

10. Out Of The Frying Pan...

"Marlowe," Jen huffed. The sound of her shoes splashing in the putrid water gradually became less repetitive. She slowed from a run, to a jog, and then to a complete stop. Doubled over, she begged her heart to stop its hammering inside her chest.

"What are you doing?!? Come on!" Marlowe commanded from over her shoulder. "We've got to go!"

"I need... minute..." Jen gasped.

Marlowe stopped about ten yards away from Jen and turned around. "We don't have a minute!"

"I need one anyway..."

Marlowe stalked back toward her. Furiously, she slung the green duffel bag around to her front and dug through it. "Here," she said as she offered Jen a dose of AMP.

"You know I can't use that," she said.

"Now's not the time for your Twelve Steps garbage," Marlowe said, stepping closer and waving the AMP in Jen's face.

Jen slapped the inhaler away. "Those are formulated for you, stupid!" She snapped. "I don't feel like dying today, thank you!"

Marlowe took a step back. Despite the severity of the situation, she knew she was pushing a button that shouldn't be pushed. She sighed as she placed the AMP back in the bag.

"Well, bad news," she said, "You're probably going to get executed when they find us, so you're gonna die regardless."

Suddenly, Marlowe screamed and slammed her fist into the concrete wall of the ancient drainage tunnel, chipping away at a long-forgotten gang's graffiti.

"Fuck me," she whispered, licking blood from her knuckles. "I never should have dragged you into this."

Jen stood and leaned against the tunnel wall. Her breathing was stabilizing. "You had no choice," she said. "I'm your sister, Marlowe. I get it."

"Adopted sister, remember?"

Jen scowled. "Enough with that shit."

"Considering recent events, it might be good to start saying it again. Deny any connection to me."

"Stop it. We're not twelve years old, and this isn't school. Besides, this isn't your fault."

"Yeah," Marlowe said, "I was starting to feel bad about sending your idiot boyfriend out there to face those goons, but you're right. He's the one to blame for this."

Jen looked up at Marlowe, eyes watery, a scowl stamped across her face.

"Don't look at me like that! I didn't think they'd kill him!" Marlowe snapped. "I thought the worst they'd do is throw a collar on him and put him on trial."

"Marlowe..."

"Maybe use him as some sort of lesson for anyone considering helping me," she continued. "Well, I guess they *did* do that, didn't they..."

"I called it in," Jen said.

Marlowe's eyes grew wide. "You WHAT?!?"

"I'm sorry!" Jen pleaded. "I thought it was the only way to save you!"

Marlowe scowled. "You thought the only way to save a fugitive on the run for treason was to call in two squads of MilSec soldiers and a cybernetically enhanced 'Next Top Soldier contestant?"

"Well, no... But yes?" Jen said. She stepped toward Marlowe. "He's a Private who visits the Subs and loves cards and AMP. I dump money to in poker games to guarantee favors! I was calling one in... I thought he'd cover for us and help you out! I didn't know he would call in the calvary! I am so sorry! I didn't think--"

"You're right! You didn't think!" Marlowe yelled, taking two steps backward. "You just...reacted! Like you always do! You didn't think some plucky Private would see brand new stripes on his arm as a reward for bringing me in! You didn't think they'd be monitoring the coms! You didn't think at all! Hell, I saw the reward they have on me... I doubt you'd mind coming across an easy million credits"

"Fuck you, Marlowe!" Jen screamed. "I'd NEVER sell you out!"

"You literally just did!" Marlowe said. "You are always thinking of yourself first!"

"Oh, look who's fucking talking!" Jen said. "We've just run nearly a mile through who-know's-what's been sitting in this tunnel for who-knows-how-long because YOU--"

Jen suddenly froze. Her eyes took on a slight glow. "Oh shit!" She exclaimed. She raised her hands and began gesturing, cycling through a series of alerts that had just appeared on her HUD.

"What?" Marlowe asked urgently.

"We're near the end of the tunnel...I just reconnected to the Net," Jen said, reading each alert. "It's dad!"

"What?!? Is he ok?"

Jen tapped the air with her index finger. "He's in custody...they arrested him!" She flicked upward with her finger. She gasped. Her eyes dimmed slightly as she looked at Marlowe. "They're saying he orchestrated your escape, using his connections in MilSec. They're charging him with treason!"

"WHAT?!"

Jen gestured in the air, flicking her hands up and tapping the air as she navigated. "They're saying he was complicit in helping the traitors who sprung you...oh god, they're calling an emergency trial in front of the tribunal! Nine AM tomorrow!"

"They can't...he can't even walk or feed himself! How the hell would he have orchestrated anything-- SHIT! Jen! Get down!" Marlowe yelled, pointing at a drone that had just buzzed in from the far end of the tunnel.

Jen wasn't one for taking orders, but she knew that if Marlowe said "Get down" it was better to just do it and find out why later. She hit the deck as Marlowe picked up the chunk of rock she had chipped from the tunnel wall during her tantrum. Without her Pod, the targeting systems linking her eyes to her muscle fibers were useless. But necessity is the mother of invention, and anything can fly in a straight line if thrown hard enough. She reared back and chucked the rock with all her might, pegging the drone's left propeller. It buzzed and lurched to its side, crashed into the wall, and fell to the floor of the tunnel.

"Nice shot!" Jen remarked as she lifted herself from the muck.

"Pure luck," Marlowe said.

"Was it one of MilSec's? Do you think it saw us?"

"Probably. And probably. Doesn't matter...someone somewhere is going to wonder why it went dark, and they're going to follow the cookie crumbs through that opening to their wrecked drone. We need another way out."

"We passed another access port a few yards back," Jen suggested.

"You know where it goes?"

"No clue. I didn't go knocking on every hatch when I found this spot. Could be a bug-out tunnel like I had. Could be covered in rubble. There's only one way to find out."

"Fuck it," Marlowe resigned. "Anything's better than standing around here waiting to get caught. Let's go."

The sisters backtracked about fifty yards and took a right into a connecting tunnel that led to a ladder. Marlowe held up a finger. Jen froze. She ascended the ladder and pulled on the handle to the latch for the door. It wouldn't budge -- locked from the other side.

Undeterred, Marlowe simply pushed harder. The rung of the ladder she was standing on bent as the hatch began to give way. She wondered for a moment which would give first -- the ladder or the hatch. After a few seconds of intense pressure, the hatch decided it had enough. A loud PLINK sounded from above as the padlock that held the latch shut gave way and broke off.

Marlowe eased her way up and peeked through the small crack of the hatch. A soft glow emanated from a desk against the wall from the hatchway; a standalone screen was displaying security camera footage. Marlowe examined the screen and saw no one in view. The fourth panel in the bottom right showed the Feed from a camera just outside the building they were in. The footage displayed two MilSec soldiers in the process of questioning a resident of the Subs, two others setting fire to a shop across the street, and a few soldiers intermittently walking by.

She returned to the hatchway and waved Jen forward. Once her sister had scrambled up, Marlowe pointed to the screen and asked, "Can you tell where we are from that?"

Jen examined the Feeds from the cameras. "We're Krog-side," she observed. "Near the old market. I'm betting we're in Dirty Mike's shop. Bunch of knockoff counterfeit shit and weak drugs...total tourist trap. Nothing here we can really use, unless it's something heavy that you can bash these MilSec guys over the head with."

"I'm certain those aren't the only troops down here. We'd get slaughtered. There's probably a full garrison at each of the entrances and exits..."

"The ones they know about, sure," Jen said with a smirk.

Marlowe raised her eyebrows questioningly.

"We roaches know how to scatter when the lights go up," Jen answered. "If you can get us past these guys out front, I can get us out of here."

"Well, let's start looking for some heavy counterfeit crap I can use as a bat, I guess."

Jen approached the door to the office. Marlowe snapped her fingers twice, causing Jen to freeze and look back at her sister. Marlowe pointed to the screen displaying the security camera footage. The bottom-right corner showed two MilSec soldiers approaching the doorway to the shop. One shoved the butt of his rail rifle through the glass of the front door. The alarm rang out. The soldier cleared away the glass of the doorway and stepped through, followed by his partner.

Marlowe quickly scanned the area for anything useful. An ink pen, several markers, a clipboard...nothing. She felt under the desk and searched the drawers for a hidden weapon. She found nothing.

Then, Jen spotted something resting in the corner by the door. She picked it up. It was a samurai-style sword in a scabbard. She handed it to Marlowe, who drew it and examined the blade. She grabbed the handle with one hand and the blunt end of the blade with another, bending it to test its tensile strength. It bent into a crescent moon shape with little effort.

Jen shrugged. Marlowe gritted her teeth and shook her head.

Shouting could be heard in the distance. Marlowe and Jen rushed to the screen to see what was going on. Both soldiers, now inside the building, turned to see what the disturbance was. On the exterior camera's panel, several civilians were seen bum-rushing a MilSec soldier. The soldier was quickly overwhelmed. One of the soldiers in the building pointed to the other, and then pointed outside. The other soldier complied with the order and went to help the soldier outside, leaving the other to investigate the building.

Marlowe smiled. She signaled to Jen stay put, and made her way to the door of the office. Gingerly, she twisted the handle. The door cracked open. She slid out and very quietly shut the door behind her. She crouched behind some shelves at the back of the store. Taking note of her surroundings, she spotted a counterfeit action figure of herself. A fleeting glint of anger arose when she saw it, but she realized numbly that all her assets were frozen months ago. Even if the counterfeiters did pay her likeness royalties, as a felon, she'd never get to receive them.

She grabbed one of the fake plastic versions of herself off the display and tossed it to the far end of the shop. It landed with a clatter and the MilSec soldier investigating the shop flinched. He raised his rifle and pointed the mounted flashlight in the direction of the disturbance. Slowly, he crept along the aisle until he reached the end, turning the corner to the back of the store.

Suddenly, he felt a hand across his mouth and another around his chest, covering the camera mounted to his vest.

"Quiet now, Corporal," Marlowe whispered in his ear. "You know who I am?"

The soldier's eyes widened. Sweat glistened on his brow. He nodded.

"I don't want to kill you. If I did, you'd be dead. Do you believe me?" She asked. He nodded again.

"Good. Yank your battery and request permission to return for field repair, and I'll keep it that way. Deal?"

The corporal nodded once more. He reached for a pouch on his hip, flipped the cover open, and pulled on a wire until it snapped. The power to his field systems died.

Marlowe slowly removed her hand from the corporal's mouth and wrapped it around his chin, preparing to snap his neck at the first sign of non-compliance.

"Sarge, I got a problem," the corporal said.

Marlowe pressed her fingers into the skin under his jaw.

"Onboard just took a shit. Everything's gone dark," he continued. "I'm on backups. I gotta see the Chief and get it sorted."

Marlowe immediately put her hand back over his mouth. A very faint buzzing could be heard from the earpiece in his helmet.

"Granted?" Marlowe asked. He nodded in reply.

Marlowe yanked the camera from his chest with her right hand and tossed it. She then placed her free arm over his head while moving her left from his mouth to around his neck into a chokehold. The corporal passed out almost immediately.

Marlowe dragged the soldier back to Jen in the office. "I've got the dumbest plan ever," she said. "But it's all we got. Help me get him undressed."

Moments later, Marlowe was dressed in the soldier's gear, while he was clad in nothing but undershorts, a piece of tape covering his mouth, and packing twine wrapped around his wrists and ankles. The clothing hung loose on Marlowe, as the corporal was at least half again her size.

"This is actually a good thing," Jen said. "It'll cover those cuffs on your wrists and ankles, at least."

"I look like a cartoon," Marlowe said, holding her arms out to demonstrate how loosely the clothing hung on her frame.

"We can fix that," Jen answered. She began rifling through the drawer on the desk, finding a few binder clips and some tape. As quickly as she could, she performed makeshift hemming and binding on the uniform, pulling it as tight as she could.

"Nice work," Marlowe said as she examined her provisional outfit. "This isn't going to hold up to any sort of inspection, and heaven help me if we have to fight...but with the body armor on top and some luck, it should pass."

She donned the armor that lay in a pile on the floor, clamping each piece into place, and then picked up the soldier's biometrically coded rifle. It was useless to her as a firearm, but perfectly suitable for a prop. She slung the green duffle bag over her shoulder, dropped the visor on the helmet, and guided Jen at gunpoint out the door.

The Subs were in total disarray. All around, people lay dead or bound with cuffs, their illicit shops and makeshift homes ransacked. Teams of MilSec soldiers carried boxes of contraband out of the burning hovels while others guided groups of prisoners to transports. It was disproportionate and heavy-handed; quite possibly the largest domestic display of force MilSec had performed since the war. Marlowe shook her head. *This is horrific, and it's all my fault*, she thought wearily.

Jen led Marlowe away from the chaos toward a dead-end of head shops, strip clubs, and bars. Marlowe felt sick. Dead ends were not a place that anyone with any training would willingly go in enemy-occupied territory. But this was Jen's hood. She trusted her sister enough to abandon her training and follow her into the unknown.

A MilSec sergeant appeared from the doorway of a shop and headed toward them. Marlowe pressed the rifle into Jen's back, indicating that they should just keep walking. The sergeant waved at Marlowe, who nodded.

"What have you got here, Corporal?" The sergeant asked as he approached.

Before Marlowe could answer, Jen spat on the sergeant and yelled "Get bent, pig!"

Both surprised and pleased by her sister's improvisation, Marlowe followed her lead. She whipped the rifle around and slammed the butt of it between Jen's shoulder blades, sending her face-first to the ground. "Enough!" she yelled at Jen, who replied by raising to her knees and spitting on Marlowe's pant leg.

Marlowe looked to the sergeant, who was smirking. She pointed to her battery pack and showed him the torn wires. "Snagged while bagging this dirtbag," she said, hoping that her voice was muffled and disguised enough by the helmet mask. "Gonna drop her off and see the Chief."

"Heh, fucking Subbies," the Sergeant joked. "I'll secure her. You go get your gear fixed."

"*I've* got this, sir," Marlowe said. "This one caused me some trouble. I've got some... extra interrogating I need to do." She kicked Jen in the ribs for added effect.

The Sergeant chuckled. "Well then. Carry on, Corporal," he said with a wink.

"Yes, sir! Gladly, sir!" She answered. She kicked Jen again. "On your feet!" She ordered.

Jen looked up at Marlowe in disgust. Slowly she rose to her feet. The two resumed walking.

"Did you really have to kick me that hard?" Jen muttered over her shoulder.

"It worked, didn't it?" Marlowe replied.

"On our left," Jen said. "Sully's Bar. We need to get in there."

Jen led Marlowe to a shop in the back left corner of the dead-end. The half-burnt out sign read "Sully's."

"Get on your knees facing the doorway, and keep your hands behind your head," Marlowe said. Jen complied.

Marlowe took the bag from her shoulder and placed it beside Jen, and began rummaging through it, keeping the rifle trained on her as she did. Two MilSec soldiers passed. One nodded toward Marlowe. She nodded back.

The soldiers continued a few yards past the sisters, and then froze. They suddenly sprinted toward the shop from which Marlowe and Jen had just escaped.

"Looks like someone found our handiwork," Marlowe remarked. Jen crawled forward into the doorway and made her way to the back, behind the bar. Marlowe grabbed the duffel bag and followed close behind.

"What's in here?" Marlowe said as she ducked behind the bar with Jen.

"A way out," Jen replied. She ran her fingers under the lip of the bar, then under the first layers of shelves. "Aha!"

She pressed a button. There was a light click, and a panel in the baseboards of the wall beside them opened. Jen crawled through, followed by Marlowe. They found themselves in a tight tunnel with a ladder leading upward.

"This will put us in a bookstore at street level," Jen said as she grabbed the ladder. "No one ever shops there. Sully's own insurance plan."

"How'd you know about this?" Marlowe asked.

"I've had to use it before. Poker game. You know how it goes."

"Someone caught you cheating, huh?"

"Everyone cheats down here," Jen said. "Except, of course, off-duty MilSec guys who wander into the Subs for a wild weekend."

"And Sully saved your ass?" Marlowe asked. "He must really like you."

"Sully likes being cut in for thirty percent. Oh, and tits. He really likes tits."

Jen reached the hatch. Marlowe watched as Jen pushed lightly, testing it. It lifted with no resistance. She pushed her head up against the hatch and scanned the area. It seemed clear. She opened it fully and began to ascend. Suddenly, she shrieked as she was yanked up and out of the tunnel.

"JEN!" Marlowe yelled, clambering up the ladder as fast as she could. She leapt out of the hatch to find Jen in the arms of a burly and bald grey-bearded man who clutched a massive wrench in one of the hands also holding Jen. The two were laughing, until the man caught sight of Marlowe, clad head to toe in MilSec armor.

"MilSec! Run, Jen!" The man yelled as he lunged toward Marlowe, brandishing the pipe wrench. Marlowe caught him by the sleeve of his right arm, put her free hand around his throat, and spun him into the wall behind them.

"Marlowe!" Jen begged. "That's Sully!"

Marlowe cocked her head. She released Sully and took a step back.

Sully coughed as he rubbed his throat and regained his bearings. "Did -- cough -- Did I hear that right?" He asked. "Marlowe? As in MK?"

Jen positioned herself between the two. "It's okay," she said to Marlowe. "You can trust him. I promise."

Marlowe took off the MilSec helmet and dropped it to the floor. Sully's face was the very picture of shock. "Sully, meet my sister, Marlowe. Marlowe, this is Sully."

Marlowe smirked and tossed a half-wave, half-salute toward Sully, and then began removing the overlarge MilSec armor.

"I can't believe it..." Sully said, Marlowe Kana is your sister...?"

"Adopted," Marlowe said. Jen hit her on the shoulder.

"Well shit!" Sully said with a laugh. "I'm a huge fan! I hate MilSec, but you...you I always loved! But...how'd you end up here?"

"Long story for another time," Marlowe said, pulling her orange-jumpsuit-clad legs from the bottom portion of armor. "We've got to get out of here. You have a vehicle? Preferably pre-war?"

"Yeah, at my place. A bike and a truck," he replied. He swelled with pride as he added "Restored 'em myself!"

"Where's your place?" Jen asked.

"Other side of the Krog Street Bridge, in Peoplestown."

"Shit," Marlowe said. "I'm sure they've set up a perimeter. You see any MilSec on the streets?"

"Not really," Sully said. "But I've been here since they started torching places in the Subs...waitin' in case one of them poked their knobby heads up through the hatch there so I could knock it off!"

"Well, if they're not up here yet, they will be soon. Think you could go get the bike for us?" Marlowe asked.

"Nope," Sully answered. "But I can get the truck."

"Something wrong with the bike?" Jen asked.

"Yeah, it won't hold three people," he replied calmly.

"No fucking way," Marlowe said. "We can't afford to have you come--"

"My truck, my rules," Sully said. "Or feel free to walk."

Marlowe sighed. "Fine, whatever," she said. "Just be quick about it."

"Hot damn!" Sully said, beaming. "Okay, hunker down here, I'll be back in a jiff!" He made his way out of the back office and through the back door to the shop. The rumbling of a custom motorcycle could be heard through the walls.

"Wait, the motorcycle's already here?!? That son of a..." Marlowe said, grinding her teeth. Before she could make her way toward the door, the bike growled its way out of the back lot of the bookstore and off into the distance.

"That's Sully," Jen said with a chuckle. "Trust me, he's solid."

"He's extra weight, and we need to travel light."

"He's useful, and we need the help."

"We're about to go get some help," Marlowe said, putting her back against the wall and sliding down it until she landed gingerly on her rear. "If they're still there, that is."

"They who?"

Marlowe pulled a Battery bar from the duffel bag and unwrapped it. "My fan club," she remarked casually as she took a huge bite.

End Of Volume 1

About the Author

Joe Peacock has been writing on the internet in some form or fashion for 20 years. This is his first work of fiction, and it's scary as hell to release into the world. But he has learned a lot about writing through the process, and it has been a lot of fun working on this story. He also writes his own bios and doesn't quite know why he's doing so in the third person. He has cats and dogs and lives in Atlanta, GA.

Credits

Words and website stuff: **Joe Peacock**
Edited by: **Rowena Yow**

Vol. 1 Cover art by **Meghan Hetrick**

Website and supporting art by **Alex Monik**

Other books by Joe Peacock

Please visit your favorite ebook retailer to discover other books by Joe Peacock:

The Marlowe Kana Series
>   Volume 1 (this book)
>   Volume 2
>   Volume 3
>   Volume 4 (Coming soon!)

Mentally Incontinent: That Time I Burned Down a Hooters, That Time My Stalker Crashed on My Couch, and Nine Other Stories from My Weird Life

Everyone Deserves To Know What I Think: Collected Writing, 2003-2013

Follow Joe Peacock on Social Media:

Facebook: http://facebook.com/joepeacock
Twitter: http://twitter.com/joethepeacock
Blog: http://www.joepeacock.com/
Email: Joe@joepeacock.com

Follow Marlowe Kana on the web and read the next volume (and all future volumes) for FREE:

Read the whole book free!
Get extra art, downloads and more:

http://www.marlowekana.com/

Made in the USA
Lexington, KY
28 November 2017